THE BOY AND THE MAGICAL MONEY

KARTHIK VENUGOPAL

Have you ever wondered what you would do if you suddenly had access to magical money? Would you use it wisely, or would the temptation to indulge in every desire prove too strong? These are the questions at the heart of "The Boy and The Magic Money," a captivating tale that explores the true value of wealth and the power of choices.

In this enchanting story, we follow the journey of Jake, a young boy who stumbles upon a mysterious torn currency note with strange markings and an unusual glow. This discovery sets in motion a series of events that will challenge Jake's understanding of money, morality, and the impact of our decisions on others and ourselves. As readers, we are invited to join Jake on his adventure, experiencing firsthand the dilemmas he faces and the lessons he learns.

Money is a subject that touches all of our lives, regardless of age or background. It can open doors, fulfill dreams, and change lives. But it can also be a source of conflict, temptation, and moral dilemmas. "The Boy and The Magic Money" takes this universal theme and presents it through the eyes of a child, offering a fresh and innocent perspective on a topic that often becomes complicated and cynical in the adult world.

What sets this book apart is its unique approach to teaching valuable life lessons through an engaging narrative. Instead of lecturing readers on the dos and don'ts of financial responsibility, the story allows us to experience the consequences of different choices alongside Jake. We feel his excitement, temptations, and internal struggles as he navigates the power bestowed upon him by the magical note. This immersive approach makes the lessons more relatable and memorable, especially for younger readers encountering these concepts for the first time.

As an author, I've always been fascinated by how money shapes our lives and relationships. Growing up, I witnessed firsthand how financial decisions could bring families together or tear them apart. I saw friends make choices based on immediate gratification, only to regret them later. And I experienced my struggles with balancing wants and needs. These experiences inspired me to create a story that could help young readers understand the complexities of money and decision-making in an entertaining and enlightening way.

Throughout the book, several key themes emerge that are crucial for readers of all ages to understand. The first is the concept of empathy and generosity. When Jake encounters a homeless man early in his journey, he's faced with the opportunity to use his newfound power to help someone in need. This scenario encourages readers to consider the impact they can have on others' lives and the importance of looking beyond our own desires.

Another central theme is self-control and prioritisation. As Jake finds himself in a toy store with the ability to buy anything he wants, he must grapple with the temptation to indulge in every whim. This situation mirrors our real-world challenges when managing our resources, teaching valuable lessons about delayed gratification and the difference between wants and needs.

The book also delves into the themes of loyalty and problem-solving. When Jake's best friend finds themselves in trouble, our protagonist must figure out how to use the note's power to help without revealing its secret. This scenario highlights the importance of supporting those we care about while also respecting boundaries and using creativity to overcome obstacles.

Conflict resolution is another crucial concept explored in the story. When confronted by a school bully, Jake is presented with the opportunity to use the note for revenge. However, he must decide whether this is the right course of action or if a more positive solution can be found. This situation encourages readers to think critically about how to handle conflicts in their own lives and the potential consequences of their actions.

As the story progresses, we encounter community spirit and selfless giving themes. Jake's experiences at a local fair, where he uses the note to help various people in need, showcase the joy and fulfilment that can come from contributing to the well-being of others. This part of the story emphasises the importance of looking beyond our needs and considering how we can positively impact our communities.

Perhaps the most profound theme explored in the book is the true meaning of happiness and the value of personal growth. As Jake faces his greatest challenge – the opportunity to become incredibly wealthy – he must confront his values and question what truly brings fulfilment in life. This pivotal moment encourages readers to reflect on their own definitions of success and happiness and whether material wealth alone can provide lasting satisfaction.

While "The Boy and The Magic Money" is primarily aimed at young readers, its messages and themes resonate with audiences of all ages. For children and teenagers, the book is an engaging introduction to important life lessons about money, decision-making, and personal values. It provides a safe space to explore complex ideas and consider the consequences of choices without real-world risks.

Parents and educators will find the book a valuable tool for initiating conversations with young people about financial responsibility, ethics, and personal growth. The relatable scenarios presented in the story offer excellent jumping-off points for discussions about real-life situations and challenges.

Adult readers can benefit from the book's fresh perspective on familiar themes. In a world where financial pressures and ethical dilemmas are commonplace, the story reminds us of the simple truths we sometimes forget amidst the complexities of adult life.

By reading "The Boy and The Magic Money," readers will gain much more than just an entertaining story. They'll develop a deeper understanding of money's role in our lives and the power of our choices. The book encourages critical thinking about financial decisions, fostering skills that will serve readers well throughout their lives.

Readers will also gain insight into the importance of empathy and generosity, learning how small acts of kindness can significantly impact others and ourselves. The story promotes the development of emotional intelligence, teaching readers to consider the feelings and needs of those around them.

Furthermore, the book provides valuable lessons in self-control and prioritisation. In a world filled with

constant temptations and instant gratification, these skills are more critical than ever. Readers will learn strategies for managing impulses and making decisions that align with their long-term goals and values.

Problem-solving skills are another key takeaway from the book. As Jake navigates various challenges, readers will learn the importance of creative thinking and perseverance in overcoming obstacles. These skills are invaluable in all aspects of life, from personal relationships to academic and professional pursuits.

The book also fosters a sense of community responsibility and the joy of giving. By witnessing Jake's experiences at the community fair, readers will be inspired to consider how they can contribute to their communities and the positive impact they can have on others' lives.

Perhaps most importantly, readers will gain a new perspective on the true meaning of wealth and happiness. Through Jake's journey, they'll be encouraged to question societal norms about success and consider what truly brings fulfilment. This introspection can lead to more mindful decision-making and a greater sense of purpose.

I remember the first time I held a significant amount of money. I was twelve years old and had just received a generous birthday gift from my grandmother. The possibilities seemed endless, and I felt a mix of excitement and anxiety. What should I do with it? Should I save it for something important or spend it on something fun? As I grappled with this decision, I realised that money wasn't just about buying things – it was about choices, values, and the person I wanted to be.

This experience, and many others like it, inspired me to write "The Boy and The Magic Money." I wanted to create a story that could help young readers navigate these complex feelings and decisions, providing them with a framework for thinking about money and its role in their lives.

As you embark on this journey with Jake, I invite you to reflect on your experiences with money and your choices. Consider how Jake's lessons might apply to your life, regardless of your age or circumstances. What would you do if you found a magical note? How would you use its power? And what does true wealth mean to you?

"The Boy and The Magic Money" is more than just a story about a boy and a magical currency note. It's a mirror that reflects our own values, desires, and potential for growth. It's a guide that helps us navigate the complex financial and ethical decision-making world. And it's a reminder that the true magic in life doesn't come from money itself but from the wisdom to use it wisely and the heart to use it kindly.

As you turn the pages of this book, prepare to be entertained, challenged, and inspired. You'll laugh at Jake's misadventures, hold your breath during his moments of temptation, and cheer for him as he grows and learns.

But more than that, you'll find yourself questioning your own assumptions about money, success, and happiness. You might find yourself reconsidering that impulse purchase you were planning to make. You may look at the people around you with new eyes, wondering how you could use your resources – magical or.

otherwise – to make a positive difference in their lives. You might even start to see opportunities for kindness and generosity that you never noticed before.

This book is an invitation to embark on your own journey of discovery. Just as Jake learns valuable lessons through his encounters with the magical note, you, too, will have the opportunity to gain insights that can transform your relationship with money and enrich your life in countless ways.

So, are you ready to join Jake on his adventure? Are you prepared to confront your own values, face difficult choices, and perhaps discover a bit of magic in your own life? Then, turn the page and let the journey begin. The world of "The Boy and The Magic Money" awaits, filled with wonder, wisdom, and the potential for profound personal growth.

As you read, remember that the true magic isn't in the note itself but in the choices we make and the lives we touch. And who knows? By the time you finish this book, you might just discover that you've had a kind of magic within you all along – the power to make wise decisions, help others, and find true happiness in how you live your life.

So, take a deep breath, open your mind, and prepare to see the world of money and values through new eyes. The adventure is about to begin, and I promise you, it's one you won't soon forget. Welcome to the magical, meaningful world of "The Boy and The Magic Money." Your journey starts now.

Contents

Contents

Chapter 1

The Torn Note

A Peculiar Discovery

It was just another ordinary Tuesday afternoon when Jake's life turned unexpectedly. As he trudged home from school, his backpack heavy with homework and his mind preoccupied with the upcoming math test, he noticed something glinting in the corner of his eye. Curiosity piqued, he veered off his usual path to investigate.

A crumpled piece of paper was wedged between the cracks of the sidewalk. But this wasn't just any scrap – it was a torn currency note, and something about it seemed... different. Jake knelt, his fingers hesitating for a moment before grasping the note.

When his skin made contact with the paper, he felt a strange tingling sensation. The note seemed to pulse with an energy of its own, almost as if it were alive. Jake's eyes widened as he smoothed the creases, revealing peculiar markings etched along the edges. They weren't like anything he'd seen on regular money – intricate swirls and symbols that seemed to shift and change as he looked at them.

An Unusual Glow

But the strangest thing of all was the glow. It wasn't obvious at first, but as Jake held the note up to the fading afternoon light, he noticed a faint, ethereal shimmer within the paper. It was like the note held a miniature galaxy, stars twinkling beneath its surface.

"What in the world?" Jake muttered, glancing around to see if anyone else had noticed this bizarre occurrence. But the street remained empty, the only sound the distant barking of a neighbour's dog.

Jake's heart raced as he carefully folded the note and slipped it into his pocket. He couldn't explain why, but he felt an overwhelming urge to keep this discovery a secret. Something told him this wasn't just an ordinary currency but something far more significant.

The Journey Home

As Jake resumed his walk home, his mind buzzed with questions. Where had this note come from? What did the strange markings mean? And most importantly, why did it glow like that? He constantly reached into his pocket, checking to ensure the note was still there, half expecting it to have vanished like some sort of magical illusion.

The familiar sight of his house came into view, but for once, Jake didn't feel the usual relief of being home. Instead, a mix of excitement and apprehension swirled in his stomach. He knew that he'd have to decide what to do with his mysterious find once he stepped through that door.

A Secret to Keep

Jake's mom greeted him as he entered, her voice warm and curious. "How was school today, honey?"

For a moment, Jake considered telling her about the note. But something held him back. "It was fine," he replied, mustering up a smile. "Just a regular day."

As he climbed the stairs to his room, Jake couldn't help but feel a twinge of guilt. He'd never kept secrets from his parents before. But this... this felt different. Special. Like it was meant just for him.

Examining the Evidence

Once safely in his room, Jake carefully withdrew the note from his pocket. In the privacy of his own space, he allowed himself to examine his find. The note was unlike any currency he'd ever seen. The paper felt different—softer, almost silky to the touch. And the design... it was both familiar and alien at the same time.

Jake traced his finger along the intricate markings, feeling that same tingle of energy. As he did so, the glow intensified, casting a soft, warm light across his desk. It was beautiful and slightly unnerving at the same time.

"What are you?" Jake whispered, more to himself than to the note. Of course, it didn't answer. But as he stared at it, Jake couldn't shake the feeling that this was just the beginning of something much bigger.

A Decision to Make

As the afternoon wore on, Jake could not focus on anything else. His homework lay forgotten on his desk, his favourite video game untouched, all he could think about was the note and what it might mean.

Should he tell someone? His parents? His best friend, Tom? Or should he keep it a secret and try to unravel its mystery alone? His responsible part knew that he should probably hand it over to the authorities. After all, it was technically lost property. But another part of him, which craved adventure and excitement, wanted to hold onto it.

As Jake lay in bed that night, the note safely tucked under his pillow, he made a decision. He would keep the note, at least for now. He would try to understand its secrets, to figure out why it had come into his possession. Something told him this wasn't a coincidence – that he was meant to find this note for a reason.

Dreams of Possibility

Jake's dreams were filled with swirling colours and strange symbols that night. He saw himself using the note in various ways—helping people, solving problems, and even flying through the air like a superhero.

The dreams faded quickly when he woke the next morning, but the sense of excitement and possibility remained.

Jake carefully tucked the note into a hidden pocket in his backpack as he got ready for school. He couldn't explain why, but he needed to keep it close. Whatever this note was, whatever power it held, Jake knew that his life was about to change in ways he couldn't even imagine.

The First Test

Little did Jake know that his first test would come sooner than expected. As he walked to school, his mind still buzzing with thoughts of the magical note, he encountered a sight that would set his adventure truly in motion.

Ahead of him, huddled in the doorway of a closed shop, was a homeless man. Jake had seen him around the neighbourhood before but had never paid much attention. Today, however, something made him pause.

The man looked up as Jake approached, his eyes weary but kind. "Spare any change, young man?" he asked, his voice rough but not unkind.

Jake felt the weight of the note in his pocket. For a moment, he was tempted to keep walking, to save the note for something more important. But then he remembered the strange energy he'd felt, the sense that this note was meant for something special.

With slightly trembling hands, Jake reached into his pocket and pulled out the note. As he held it out to the man, he noticed the glow intensifying as if approving of his decision.

The homeless man's eyes widened as he saw the note. "Are you sure, lad?" he asked, disbelief clear in his voice.

Jake nodded, feeling a warmth spread through him as the man carefully took the note. Jake felt a spark of energy pass between them as their hands touched.

"Thank you," the man said, his voice thick with emotion. "You've no idea what this means,"

As Jake continued to school, he felt lighter, as if he'd passed some sort of test. He didn't know what would happen next, but he had a feeling that this was just the beginning of a much bigger adventure.

A New Perspective

The interaction with the homeless man stayed with Jake throughout the school day. He found himself paying more attention to the people around him, wondering about their stories and struggles. Had the note somehow opened his eyes to the world in a new way?

During lunch, his best friend Tom noticed his distraction. "You okay, Jake? You seem a million miles away."

Jake considered telling Tom about the note and the strange encounter that morning. But something held him back. Not because he didn't trust Tom but because he felt like he needed to figure out this on his own, at least for now.

"I'm fine," Jake replied with a smile. "Just thinking about some stuff."

Tom shrugged, accepting the answer, and launched into a story about his new video game. Jake listened, but part of his mind remained on the magical note and what it might mean for his future.

The Power of Kindness

As the final bell rang and Jake headed home, he took a different route, passing by where he'd met the homeless man that morning. To his surprise, the man was still there, but something had changed. He was standing taller, with a small smile, as he chatted with a passerby.

When he spotted Jake, the man's face lit up. "There you are, my young friend!" he called out. "I wanted to thank you again. Your kindness... it's changed everything."

Jake approached cautiously, curious but also a little wary. "What do you mean?"

The man's eyes twinkled. "That note you gave me... it was more than just money. It gave me hope. And with that hope, I found the strength to make some changes. I've got a job interview tomorrow, my first in years."

Jake felt a warmth spread through him, a sense of pride and accomplishment unlike anything he'd experienced. Could this be the true power of the note? Not just its mysterious glow or strange markings, but its ability to inspire change and hope?

A Growing Mystery

As Jake continued home, his mind raced with new questions. How had the note known to guide him towards helping the homeless man? Was it somehow sentient, able to influence events? Or was it simply a catalyst, bringing out the best among those who possessed it?

One thing was becoming clear—this note was far more than just magical currency. It seemed to have the power to change lives and inspire kindness and generosity. And somehow, it had chosen Jake as its keeper.

Back in his room, Jake pulled out a notebook and began to jot down everything he knew about the note so far: its appearance, the strange markings, the glow, and now its apparent ability to inspire positive change. He felt he'd greatly add to this list in the coming days.

The Call to Adventure

As Jake sat at his desk, staring at the list he'd made, he felt excitement and trepidation. Part of him wanted to hide the note away, to return to his normal life of school, friends, and video games. But a larger part, the part that had always dreamed of adventure and making a difference in the world, knew that wasn't an option.

This note, whatever it was, had come into his life for a reason. It had already shown him the power of kindness and had opened his eyes to the struggles of others. What else could it teach him? What other changes could it bring about?

Jake made a decision then and there. He would embrace this adventure wherever it might lead. He would use the note's power responsibly, learning its secrets and trying to understand its purpose. And maybe, just maybe, he could make the world a little bit better in the process.

Preparing for the Unknown

With his mind made up, Jake began to prepare. He dug out an old backpack from his closet, one small enough to carry around without drawing attention. In it, he packed a few essentials – a water bottle, snacks, and a small first aid kit. He wasn't sure what he might need on this adventure, but it felt good to be prepared.

Next, he created a secret compartment in the backpack, a hidden pocket where he could safely store the note. Jake couldn't help but feel like a character in one of his favourite adventure stories as he worked.

Except this wasn't fiction – this was real, and he was the hero of this tale.

The Promise of Tomorrow

As night fell and Jake prepared for bed, he was filled with a nervous energy. Tomorrow would

be the start of something new, something exciting and potentially life-changing. He had no idea what challenges he might face, what decisions he'd have to make. But he felt ready, or as ready as he could be.

Lying in bed, Jake whispered a quiet promise to himself and the mysterious note. "I don't know why you chose me," he said softly, "but I promise to use your power wisely. To help people learn and grow. Whatever adventure you have in store for me, I'm ready."

With those words, Jake drifted to sleep, his dreams filled with glowing notes, kind strangers, and the promise of adventures. Little did he know how much his life would change or the incredible journey that awaited him in the days ahead.

A New Dawn

The next morning, Jake woke with a sense of purpose he'd never felt before. As he got ready for school, he was aware of the note, safely hidden in his backpack. It felt like a secret superpower, a responsibility, and an opportunity all rolled into one.

As he headed out the door, his mom said, "Have a good day at school, honey!"

Jake turned and smiled. "Thanks, Mom. I have a feeling it's going to be a great day." And he meant it. Because today wasn't just another school day – it was the first day of his grand adventure.

The Journey Begins

As Jake set off down the sidewalk, he couldn't help but look at his familiar neighbourhood with new eyes. Every person he passed, every house and shop seemed to hold the potential for mystery and magic. He wondered about the stories behind each face he saw, the challenges and triumphs hidden behind closed doors.

The backpack's weight on his shoulders reminded him of the incredible secret he carried. With each step, Jake felt a mix of excitement and nervousness. What would happen today? Would the note reveal more of its powers? Would he face another test of character?

One thing was certain – life would never be the same again. Jake had stepped into a world of magic and mystery, and there was no turning back. As he approached the school gates, he took a deep breath, squared his shoulders, and stepped forward into his new adventure.

The torn note had set everything in motion, and Jake was ready to embrace whatever came next. Little did he know, this was just the beginning of a journey that would challenge him, change him, and ultimately reveal the true magic in the world – and within himself.

The Classroom Revelation

As Jake settled into his seat for the day's first class, he couldn't help but feel like he was living a double life.

On the surface, he was just another student, surrounded by the familiar sights and sounds of the classroom. But beneath it all, he was the keeper of a magical secret, embarking on an adventure beyond his wildest dreams.

Ms. Thompson, his English teacher, began the lesson with a quote: "Magic is believing in yourself. If you can do that, you can make anything happen." Jake's ears perked up at the word 'magic'. Was it a coincidence, or was the universe trying to tell him something?

As Ms. Thompson discussed the power of belief and imagination in literature, Jake found himself drawing parallels to his own situation. The note had shown him that there was more to the world than met the eye. It had made him believe in the impossible. And now, sitting in this ordinary classroom, he realised that maybe the real magic wasn't just in the note itself but in how it was changing his perception of the world.

A Lunchtime Dilemma

When lunchtime rolled around, Jake found himself faced with an unexpected dilemma. Standing in the cafeteria line, he overheard a conversation between two younger students ahead of him.

"I forgot my lunch money again," one of them said, his voice tinged with embarrassment and worry. "Mom's going to be so mad."

Jake felt a familiar warmth in his pocket, where he kept his own lunch money. He knew the note was safely in his backpack, but its presence radiated through him, urging him to act. Without hesitation, Jake tapped the younger student on the shoulder.

"Hey," he said, offering a friendly smile. "I've got some extra money. Why don't you use it for lunch today?"

The look of relief and gratitude on the younger student's face was all the reward Jake needed. He felt that now-familiar surge of warmth and rightness as he handed over the money. It wasn't the grand gesture of giving the magical note to the homeless man, but it was a reminder that kindness could be found in small, everyday actions, too.

The Ripple Effect

Jake didn't realise that his simple act of kindness had set off a chain reaction. Buoyed by this unexpected generosity, the younger student went on to share his dessert with a classmate who was having a bad day. That classmate, in turn, was inspired to help another student with a complex math problem.

By the end of the lunch period, the atmosphere in the cafeteria had subtly shifted. There was more laughter, more sharing, more open smiles. Jake, observing all this from his table, felt a sense of awe. Had his small act of kindness, inspired by the magical note, really caused all this?

It was a powerful lesson – magic didn't always have to be grand or obvious. Sometimes, it could be

It is as simple as a kind word or a helping hand, creating ripples that spread far beyond the initial act.

An Unexpected Challenge

As the school day neared its end, Jake faced an unexpected challenge. During the last period, Mr Davis announced a pop quiz in math, Jake's least favourite subject. A collective groan went up from the class, and Jake felt his stomach sink.

For a brief, wild moment, he wondered if the magical note could help him ace the quiz. But as quickly as the thought came, he dismissed it. That wouldn't be right. It wouldn't be fair to his classmates, and more importantly, it wouldn't be true to the spirit of what he was learning about the note's power.

Instead, Jake took a deep breath and focused. He remembered all the study sessions with his dad, all the practice problems he'd worked through. As he looked at the quiz paper, he realised that he knew more than he thought he did. The answers didn't come easily, but they came.

When he handed in his quiz, Jake felt a sense of accomplishment that had nothing to do with magic and everything to do with his efforts. This was another important lesson—that while the note could inspire and guide, true growth and achievement came from within.

The Walk Home

As Jake left school that afternoon, his mind buzzed with everything that had happened. It had been just a normal school day on the surface, but underneath, it felt like he had learned more about the note – and himself – than he had in any class.

He took a different route home, partly out of a sense of adventure and partly hoping he might encounter another opportunity to use the note's power for good. As he walked, he noticed things he'd never noticed before – the way the sunlight filtered through the leaves, the sounds of birds singing, the smiles exchanged between passersby.

Was this another effect of the note? This heightened awareness, this more profound appreciation for the world around him? Or was it simply that he was learning to look at the world with new eyes, to see the magic in the everyday?

A Moment of Reflection

Halfway home, Jake came across a small park he'd never noticed. Drawn by its peaceful atmosphere, he took a break, sitting on a bench beneath a sprawling oak tree. He pulled out the magical note, carefully shielding it from view.

The note seemed to shimmer even more than usual in the dappled sunlight. The strange markings along its edge seemed to dance and shift as if trying to tell him something. Jake traced them with his finger, wondering about their meaning, the note's origin, and why it had chosen him.

"What are you trying to teach me?" he whispered to the note. Of course, it didn't answer, at least not in words. But as a gentle breeze rustled the leaves above him, Jake felt a sense of peace and purpose. He knew he was on the right path, whatever this journey was, whatever challenges lay ahead.

The Promise of Adventure

As the sun began to set, casting long shadows across the park, Jake knew it was time to head home. He carefully tucked the note back into its hiding place and stood up, stretching his legs.

Looking around the park one last time, Jake felt excited. This was just the beginning. Who knew what tomorrow might bring? What new lessons might he learn, and what opportunities to help others might arise?

One thing was certain – life would never be boring again. Not with this magical note as his guide, not with this newfound awareness of the world around him. As Jake set off towards home, he couldn't help but smile. Whatever adventures lay ahead, he was ready to face them.

A Family Evening

When Jake arrived home, he found his parents in the kitchen, preparing dinner together. The familiar scene of domestic harmony struck him differently today. He saw the love in their gestures, the teamwork in their actions, the joy they took in each other's company. Had these things always been there, and he'd just never noticed?

"How was school, honey?" his mom asked, stirring a pot on the stove.

For a moment, Jake was tempted to tell them everything – about the note, the homeless man, and the lessons he was learning. But something held him back, not out of distrust, but out of a sense that this was his journey to navigate, at least for now.

"It was good," he said instead, smiling. "I learned a lot today."

And it wasn't a lie. He had learned more today than he could have imagined when he woke up this morning.

Nighttime Reflections

That night, as Jake lay in bed, he found himself unable to sleep. His mind was too full of the day's events and possibilities. He pulled out the notebook where he'd been recording his experiences with the magical note and began to write.

He wrote about the homeless man and the lesson in kindness, the ripple effect of generosity in the school cafeteria, facing challenges with his own abilities rather than relying on magic, and seeing the world with new eyes.

As he wrote, Jake began to see patterns emerging. The note wasn't just about magic or helping people.

It was about growth, learning to see the best in himself and others, and positively impacting the world around him.

Dreams of What's to Come

Finally, as the first light of dawn began to creep through his window, Jake drifted off to sleep. His dreams were vivid and colourful, filled with images of the note glowing brightly, people helping each other, and a world transformed by kindness and understanding.

In his dreams, Jake saw himself facing challenges he couldn't even imagine – standing up to bullies, solving mysteries, and making difficult choices. But in each scenario, he felt the comforting presence of the note, not solving his problems for him but giving him the strength and wisdom to face them himself.

A New Day Dawns

When Jake's alarm went off a few hours later, he woke with a start, the dreams still vivid. He felt excitement and nervousness as he got ready for another school day. What would today bring? What new lessons would he learn? What opportunities to help others would arise?

As he headed out the door, his backpack slung over his shoulder and the magical note safely tucked away inside, Jake felt ready for whatever the day might bring. He had taken the first steps on an incredible journey and couldn't wait to see where it would lead him next.

The torn note had opened his eyes to a world of possibilities and shown him the magic in everyday kindness and personal growth. And this was just the beginning. As Jake set off the sidewalk, he knew his greatest adventures were still to come.

Chapter 2

The First Test

As Jake clutched the mysterious torn note in his hand, its strange markings and unusual glow still fresh in his mind, he couldn't shake the feeling that something extraordinary was about to happen. Little did he know that his first test was just around the corner.

An Unexpected Encounter

Jake rounded the corner of his neighbourhood, his mind swirling with questions about the peculiar currency he had discovered. Suddenly, he came face to face with a sight that made him stop. There, huddled against the wall of an old building, was a man who looked like he hadn't had a proper meal or a warm bed in weeks.

The man's clothes were tattered and dirty, his beard unkempt, and his eyes weary with exhaustion. As Jake approached, the man looked up, and their eyes met. At that moment, Jake felt a strange warmth emanating from the note in his pocket.

The Inner Struggle

I remember the first time I encountered someone in need on the street. It's a moment that sticks with you, isn't it? You're suddenly faced with a reality far removed from your own and unsure how to react. That's precisely where Jake found himself.

He stood there, frozen, as a battle raged within him. On one hand, he wanted to help. The man's suffering was palpable, and Jake's heart ached at the sight. But on the other hand, he was just a kid. What could he do? And more importantly, should he use this magical note he had just found?

Jake had always been taught to be cautious with strangers, and here he was, contemplating using a mysterious, potentially magical object to help one. The conflict between his desire to help and his uncertainty about the consequences weighed heavily on him.

The Voice of Empathy

As Jake stood there, wrestling with his thoughts, he remembered something his grandmother once told him:

"Empathy is the ability to put yourself in someone else's shoes. It's what makes us human."

Looking at the homeless man, Jake tried to imagine what it would be like to be in his position: cold, hungry, and alone. People would walk by daily, averting their eyes, pretending not to see him. The thought made Jake's heart clench.

At that moment, he realised that the magical note might have led him here for a reason. Perhaps this was his chance to make a real difference in someone's life.

The Decision

With a deep breath, Jake reached into his pocket and pulled out the note. As he did, he noticed something strange. The markings on the note seemed to shift and change, and suddenly, in place of the usual denomination, he saw the words "Hot Meal and Warm Bed."

Jake blinked in surprise. Was this the note's magic at work? He looked from the note to the man again, realising this was no coincidence. The note was giving him exactly what he needed to help.

With newfound determination, Jake approached the man. "Excuse me, sir," he said, his voice trembling slightly. "I... I'd like to help you if that's okay."

The man looked up, surprised and with a hint of suspicion in his eyes. "Help me? How?" Jake held out the note. "This... this is for you. It's for a hot meal and a warm bed."

The Power of Generosity

As the man hesitantly took the note, something remarkable happened. The paper seemed to glow for a moment, and then, right before Jake's eyes, it transformed into a voucher for a local shelter, complete with details for a meal and a night's stay.

The man's eyes widened in disbelief. "I... I don't know what to say. Thank you, young man. You have no idea what this means to me."

Jake felt a warmth spread through his chest, a feeling of joy and satisfaction that he had never experienced before. He realised this was the power of generosity, the incredible feeling that comes from helping others without expecting anything in return.

The Lesson Learned

As Jake watched the man gather his belongings and head towards the shelter, he reflected on what had just happened. He had been given a choice - to ignore someone in need or to take a risk and help. By choosing empathy and generosity, he had made a difference in someone's life and learned something profound about himself.

You see, sometimes the greatest life lessons come from the most unexpected places. Jake had started his day as an ordinary boy and ended it, understanding the extraordinary power of kindness and compassion.

The Ripple Effect

What Jake didn't realise at that moment was that his act of kindness would have far-reaching consequences. The man he helped, George, would never forget the young boy who showed him kindness when he needed it most.

George would go on to turn his life around, inspired by Jake's generosity. He would eventually find a job, get back on his feet, and dedicate his life to helping other homeless individuals.

It all started with one small act of kindness: one boy who chose to listen to his heart and use his newfound magical ability to help others.

Reflection and Growth

Jake couldn't stop thinking about what had happened as he walked home that evening. He had always thought of himself as a good person, but today, he had been put to the test. And at that moment of decision, he had discovered a strength and compassion within himself that he didn't know existed.

He thought about how easy it would have been to walk past George and pretend he hadn't seen him. Many people did just that every day. By choosing to help, Jake has not only changed George's life but also changed something within himself.

The Magic Within

As night fell and Jake prepared for bed, he again took out the magical note. To his surprise, it had returned to its original form, the strange markings and glow just as mysterious as before.

But now, Jake understood something important about the note's magic. It wasn't just about the physical transformations or the ability to provide what was needed. The real magic was in the way it opened his eyes to the needs of others and gave him the courage to act.

A New Perspective

As Jake drifted off to sleep that night, he saw the world differently. When he thought of his neighbourhood, he no longer saw just buildings and streets. He saw people—individuals with their own stories, struggles, and needs.

He realised that everyone, no matter their circumstances, deserved kindness and compassion. More importantly, he understood that he had the power to make a difference, whether magical note or not.

The Journey Ahead

As Jake closed his eyes, he couldn't help but wonder what other challenges and opportunities the magical note might bring. He had passed his first test, but something told him this was just the beginning of a bigger adventure.

Little did he know that his next challenge would come sooner than he expected, testing not just his compassion but also his self-control and ability to prioritise. But that, dear reader, is a story for another chapter.

For now, Jake slept soundly, his heart full of the warmth that comes from knowing you've made a positive difference in the world. And as he slept, the magical note glowed softly in his pocket, ready for whatever adventure tomorrow might bring.

The Power of Small Actions

It's easy to think that we need to make big, grand gestures to make a difference in the world. But Jake's experience shows us that sometimes, it's the small actions that have the biggest impact.

Think about it. All Jake did was offer a meal and a bed to someone in need. It wasn't a huge sacrifice on his part, but to George, it meant everything. It was a lifeline, a glimmer of hope in what must have felt like a very dark time.

And that's the beauty of kindness and generosity. They have a ripple effect that extends far beyond the initial action. Jake's simple act of kindness helped George in that moment and set him on a path to turn his life around and help others.

Empathy in Action

Jake's encounter with George is a perfect example of empathy in action. Empathy isn't just about feeling sorry for someone. It's about truly putting yourself in their shoes, understanding their struggles, and then Taking action to help.

When Jake looked at George, he didn't just see a homeless man. He saw a fellow human being who was struggling, someone who needed help and kindness. And instead of just feeling bad and walking away, Jake chose to act on that empathy.

This is a powerful lesson for all of us. How often do we see someone in need and think, "That's so sad," but then continue on with our day? Jake shows us that true empathy requires action.

The Courage to Help

It's worth noting that what Jake did took courage. As a young boy, approaching a stranger on the street, especially one in George's condition, must have been intimidating. Many adults would hesitate in a similar situation.

But Jake pushed past his fear because he knew it was the right thing to do. This teaches us an important lesson about courage. Being brave isn't about not feeling fear; it's about doing what's right even when you are afraid.

The Magic of Giving

One of the most beautiful aspects of Jake's experience is how it affected him. Yes, he helped George, but in the process, he also discovered something wonderful about himself. He experienced the joy and satisfaction that comes from helping others.

I've experienced this in my life, and I bet you have, too. A unique kind of happiness comes from giving, from knowing that you've made someone else's life a little bit better. It's a feeling that no amount of money or material possessions can be replicated.

Learning to See Need

Jake's encounter with George opened his eyes to the needs around him. This is such an important skill to develop. In our busy lives, it's easy to become blind to the struggles of others. We rush from place to place, focused on our problems and goals, often missing the opportunities to help right in front of us.

But once you start looking and training yourself to see a need, you'll be amazed at how many opportunities there are to make a difference. It could be as simple as helping a neighbour carry their groceries or as involved as volunteering at a local charity. The key is to keep your eyes and your heart open.

The Responsibility of Ability

Jake's magical note gave him the ability to help uniquely. But with that ability came responsibility. He had to decide how to use this power, whether to use it selfishly or to help others.

This is true for all of us. We all have abilities, skills, and resources that we can use to help others. It might not be a magical note, but it could be your time, skills, knowledge, or resources. The question is, how will you use what you have?

The Test of Character

In many ways, Jake's encounter with George tested his character. It revealed who he truly was when faced with a difficult decision, and Jake passed that test with flying colours.

But here's the thing about tests of character - they don't just reveal who we are; they shape who we become. By choosing to help George, Jake wasn't just showing his compassion, he was strengthening it. He was becoming more of the person he wanted to be.

This is how character is built—not through grand, heroic deeds but through the small choices we make every day. Each time we choose kindness over indifference or generosity over selfishness, we're shaping our character and becoming better versions of ourselves.

The Importance of Awareness

Jake's experience highlights the importance of being aware of our surroundings and the people in them. In our increasingly digital world, it's easy to walk down the street with our eyes glued to our phones, oblivious to what's happening around us.

But when we do that, we miss opportunities to connect, help, and make a difference. Jake could have easily walked past George without noticing him. But because he was aware and present, he could see the need and respond to it.

This is a valuable lesson for all of us. By being more present and aware in our daily lives, we open ourselves up to more opportunities to help others and positively impact the world around us.

The Power of Choice

Ultimately, the power of choice stands out most about Jake's experience. When faced with the opportunity to help, Jake could have chosen to walk away. He could have decided it wasn't his problem or that he was too young to make a difference.

But he didn't. He chose to help. He chose compassion over indifference, action over inaction. And that choice made all the difference.

This is a reminder that we all have this power. Every day, we face choices that allow us to help others or focus solely on ourselves. The cumulative effect of these choices shapes not just our own lives but the world around us.

Looking Ahead

As we leave Jake at the end of this chapter, we can see how this experience has changed him. He's not Just a boy with a magical note anymore. He's a boy who has discovered the power of kindness, the importance of empathy, and the joy of helping others.

These lessons will serve him well as he faces new challenges and opportunities in the coming chapters. They also serve as valuable reminders for all of us as we navigate our lives and encounter others.

Remember, like Jake, we all have the power to make a difference. We all can choose kindness, act with empathy, and help those in need. In doing so, we not only change the lives of others but also discover the best versions of ourselves.

As we move forward, let's carry these lessons with us. Let's strive to be more aware, compassionate, and willing to act when needed. Because, in the end, it's not about having magical powers. It's about recognising the magic in simple acts of kindness and the power we all have to make the world a little bit better, one small action at a time.

Chapter 3

The Tempting Toy Store

As Jake walked home from school, the magical note tucked safely in his pocket, he couldn't help but feel a mixture of excitement and trepidation. The encounter with the homeless man had opened his eyes to the power of the note, but it had also left him with more questions than answers. Little did he know that his next challenge was just around the corner.

The Glowing Invitation

Jake was about to turn onto his street when he noticed something odd. The note in his pocket began to glow, pulsing with a soft, warm light. Curious, he pulled it out and watched as the strange markings on its surface seemed to shift and change. Suddenly, an invisible force tugged at the note, pulling it gently in the direction of the town centre.

"What now?" Jake muttered to himself, both excited and nervous about what this could mean.

Following the note's lead, Jake found himself walking down Main Street, past familiar shops and bustling cafes. The note's glow intensified as he approached a store he had never paid much attention to before - Wondrous Wares Toy Emporium.

A Toy Lover's Paradise

As Jake pushed open the heavy wooden door, a tinkling bell announced his arrival. The sight that greeted him took his breath away. Floor to ceiling, the store was packed with every imaginable toy. Model trains chugged along tracks that wound through miniature landscapes, remote-controlled planes zoomed overhead, and shelves upon shelves were stacked with board games, action figures, and stuffed animals of all shapes and sizes.

The air was thick with the scent of new plastic and fresh paint, mingled with the sweet aroma of cotton candy from a nearby machine. Soft, whimsical music played in the background, adding to the magical atmosphere.

Jake's eyes widened as he took it all in. "Wow," he whispered, his earlier worries momentarily forgotten in the face of this wonderland.

The Temptation Begins

As Jake wandered through the aisles, the magical note in his pocket seemed to hum with energy. He noticed that every price tag he looked at suddenly appeared affordable, no matter how expensive the item actually was. It was as if the note offered him the chance to buy everything in the store.

Jake's heart raced as he realised the implications. With this note, he could have any toy he wanted. He could buy out the entire store if he wished. The thought was both thrilling and overwhelming.

He picked up a state-of-the-art gaming console, one he had been eyeing for months but could never afford. The price tag shimmered and changed before his eyes, now showing a sum that was well within his reach. Jake's hand trembled as he held the box, torn between desire and an uneasy feeling in the pit of his stomach.

The Voice of Reason

As Jake stood there, contemplating whether to make the purchase, a small voice in the back of his mind spoke up. It sounded suspiciously like his mother's voice, reminding him of the value of money and the importance of making wise choices.

"Jake," the voice seemed to say, "remember that just because you can buy something doesn't mean you should. Think about what you really need, not just what you want."

Jake set the gaming console back on the shelf, his brow furrowed in thought. He realised that this was another test, perhaps even more challenging than the one with the homeless man. This time, the note wasn't asking him to be generous to others but to exercise self-control and make responsible decisions for himself.

The Parade of Desires

Determined to explore further, Jake continued his journey through the store. Each aisle presented new temptations, each more alluring than the last. He found himself picking up item after item, marvelling at how the prices always adjusted to seem reasonable and affordable.

There was a lifelike robot dog that could perform tricks and respond to voice commands. A massive LEGO set that could build an entire city. A professional-grade telescope that could show the rings of Saturn. Each item called out to Jake, promising hours of fun and excitement.

But with each temptation, Jake forced himself to pause and think. Did he really need these things?

Would they truly make him happier in the long run? Or were they just momentary desires that would lose their appeal once obtained?

The Collector's Corner

As Jake rounded a corner, he found himself in a section of the store he had never seen before. A sign overhead read "Collector's Corner," and the shelves here were filled with rare and valuable items.

The walls were lined with vintage action figures still in their original packaging, limited-edition comic books, and one-of-a-kind collectables.

Jake's eyes were drawn to a particular item—a mint-condition first edition of his favourite comic book series. It was encased in a protective sleeve, and the cover art was as vibrant as the day it was printed. Jake had heard about this comic before; it was worth a small fortune and highly sought after by collectors worldwide.

The price tag on the comic flickered, showing a significant sum but not impossible with the power of the magical note. Jake's hand reached out almost involuntarily, his fingertips brushing the protective case.

The Weight of Choice

As Jake stood there, the comic book in his hands, he felt the weight of the decision before him. This wasn't just any toy or game; this was a genuine collector's item that could potentially increase in value over time. He could justify this purchase as an investment, couldn't he?

But even as he thought this, Jake knew he was rationalising. He wanted this comic book because it was rare and exclusive, not because he needed it or because it would bring him lasting joy. He already had plenty of comics at home that he loved and reread often.

With a heavy sigh, Jake carefully placed the comic book back on the shelf. As he did so, he felt a sense of relief washing over him. He had faced a major temptation and resisted it. The magical note in his pocket seemed to warm slightly as if approving of his decision.

The Wisdom of Priorities

Stepping back from the Collector's Corner, Jake took a moment to reflect on what he had learned. He realised that the note wasn't just testing his ability to resist temptation but also teaching him about priorities and the true value of things.

He thought about the homeless man he had helped earlier. How many meals could the price of that comic book have bought for people in need? How many warm blankets or pairs of shoes? The thought made Jake feel a bit ashamed of how caught up he had been in his own desires.

A Modest Choice

As Jake prepared to leave the store, he felt the magical note guided him towards a small display near the checkout counter. It was a collection of simple, classic toys—jump ropes, yo-yos, Rubik's Cubes, and the like. These toys didn't need batteries or complex instructions, and they relied on skill, imagination, and practice to be enjoyable.

Jake picked up a wooden puzzle. It had a complex interlocking design that challenged the solver to separate and reassemble the pieces. The puzzle was beautifully crafted and smooth to the touch. It came with a little booklet explaining its history and the principles behind its design.

The price was modest, easily within Jake's budget, even without the magical note's influence. As he held the puzzle, Jake felt a sense of rightness. He could enjoy this for a long time, something that would challenge his mind and improve his problem-solving skills.

The Checkout Challenge

Jake approached the checkout counter, the wooden puzzle in hand. As the cheerful cashier rang up his purchase, Jake reached into his pocket for the magical note. But as his fingers touched the paper, he hesitated.

Did he need to use the note for this? The puzzle was affordable without any magical assistance. Using the note felt like cheating like he wasn't fully embracing the lesson it was trying to teach him.

In a split-second decision, Jake pulled out his own money instead. As he handed over the bills, he felt a warmth spreading through his chest. He had made the right choice, not just in what he bought, but in how he bought it.

Lessons Learned

As Jake left the Wondrous Wares Toy Emporium, puzzle in hand and magical note still tucked away in his pocket, he felt like he had gained something far more valuable than any toy or collectable. He had learned important lessons about desire, self-control, and the true value of things.

He realised that the joy of having something often paled in comparison to the excitement of wanting it, that the most expensive or rare item wasn't necessarily the most fulfilling or enjoyable, and, most importantly, that making responsible choices with money—magical or otherwise—was a skill that would serve him well throughout his life.

Jake couldn't help but smile as he walked home, eager to tackle the challenge of his new puzzle. He had faced the temptations of the toy store and come out wiser for the experience. As the sun began to set, casting long shadows on the sidewalk, Jake wondered what other adventures and lessons the magical note had in store for him.

Little did he know, his next challenge would involve not just himself but someone very close to him. The magical note was far from done with its lessons, and Jake's journey was only beginning.

Reflection and Anticipation

That night, as Jake lay in bed, turning the wooden puzzle over in his hands, he couldn't help but reflect on the day's events. The toy store had been a test of his character and ability to resist immediate gratification and make thoughtful decisions. He felt proud of himself for passing the test but also humbled by how difficult it had been.

He thought about everything he had wanted in that store, all the toys and games that had seemed so essential at the moment. Now, those desires seemed distant and unimportant in the quiet of his room. What remained was the satisfaction of knowing he had made good choices and the enjoyment of the simple puzzle he had chosen.

As he finally solved the puzzle, separating the interlocking pieces and then reassembling them, Jake felt a sense of accomplishment that he knew would last far longer than the fleeting excitement of any expensive toy.

The magical note, tucked safely in his desk drawer, seemed to glow softly in the darkness. Jake knew that its lessons were far from over. What will tomorrow bring? What new challenges would he face? As he drifted off to sleep, his mind full of questions and possibilities, Jake couldn't help but feel excited for what was to come.

Little did he know, the note's next test would push him in ways he never expected, challenging not just his own desires, but his loyalty to those he cared about most. The adventure was only just beginning, and Jake's journey with the magical note was about to take an unexpected turn.

Chapter 4

A Friend in Need

The Unexpected Phone Call

It was a quiet Saturday afternoon when Jake's phone buzzed with an incoming call. He glanced at the screen and saw it was his best friend, Alex. With a smile, he answered, "Hey, Alex! What's up?"

But the cheerful greeting was met with a shaky voice on the other end. "Jake... I need your help. Can you come over?"

The tremor in Alex's voice sent a chill down Jake's spine. He'd never heard Alex sound so distressed in all the years they'd been friends. "Of course, I'll be right there. What's wrong?"

"I'll explain when you get here. Please hurry."

As Jake hung up, his mind raced with possibilities. What could have happened? Was Alex hurt? In trouble? He quickly grabbed his backpack, making sure the magical note was safely tucked inside, and headed out the door.

A Friend in Distress

When Jake arrived at Alex's house, he found his friend sitting on the front steps, head in hand. Alex looked up as Jake approached, and Jake could see the redness around his eyes. Alex had been crying.

"Thanks for coming," Alex said, his voice barely above a whisper.

Jake sat down next to his friend, concern etched on his face. "What's going on, Alex? You're scaring me."

Alex took a deep breath and began to explain. His parents had lost their jobs a few months ago and struggled to make ends meet. They'd kept it quiet, not wanting to worry Alex or ask for help. But now, they were facing eviction. They'd lose their home if they couldn't come up with the rent money by Monday.

Jake's heart sank as he listened to Alex's story. He thought about the magical note in his backpack. It could solve this problem in an instant. But how could he use it without revealing its secret?

The Dilemma

As Alex finished explaining, Jake found himself torn. On one hand, he had the power to help his friend immediately. The magical note could easily provide the money Alex's family needed. It would be so simple, so quick. Just a thought, and the problem would vanish.

But on the other hand, Jake knew that using the note came with its own set of challenges. How would he explain where the money came from? And more importantly, would it really be helping Alex and his family in the long run? Jake remembered the lessons he'd learned from his previous encounters with the note. Sometimes, the easy solution wasn't always the best one.

"I... I want to help," Jake said slowly, his mind still racing. "But I'm not sure how,"

Alex looked at him with hope and desperation in his eyes. "Any ideas would be great. We've tried everything we can think of."

Jake nodded, trying to buy himself some time to think. He needed to find a way to help that didn't involve magical money appearing out of nowhere. But what could a couple of kids do to raise that kind of money quickly?

Brainstorming Solutions

"Okay," Jake said, sitting up straighter. "Let's think this through. How much money do you need?" Alex sighed. "$2000. It's a lot, I know."

Jake whistled. It was a lot of money, especially for kids their age. But he wasn't going to give up. "Alright, let's break this down. What skills do we have? What resources?"

They spent the next hour brainstorming ideas. Jake was determined to find a solution that didn't involve the magical note. As they talked, he realised that this was more than money. It was about supporting his friend, about problem-solving, and about the power of community.

"What about a fundraiser?" Jake suggested suddenly. "We could organise something big, get the whole neighbourhood involved."

Alex looked sceptical. "In two days? Is that even possible?"

Jake felt a surge of determination. "We have to try. And we're not alone in this. We can ask for help."

Rallying the Troops

With a plan starting to form, Jake and Alex set to work. They called their other friends, explaining the situation and asking for help. To their surprise and relief, everyone they called was eager to pitch in.

Jake's mind was whirling with ideas. A car wash, a bake sale, a talent show - they could do it all. And with everyone helping, they might just pull it off.

Jake couldn't help but think about the magical notes in his backpack as they worked. It would be so easy to use it to solve this problem instantly. But as he watched his friends come together, working tirelessly to help Alex, he realised something important. The note might be able to create money, but it couldn't create this sense of community, friendship, and people coming together to help one of their own.

The Neighbourhood Unites

Word spread quickly through the neighbourhood. Alex's family had always been well-liked, always the first to help when someone was in need. Now, it was time for the community to give back.

Jake and his friends had a full plan by Saturday evening. Sunday would be a day of non-stop fundraising activities. They had permission to use the local community centre, and volunteers were lined up to help with everything from baking to face painting.

As Jake worked on making posters for the event, he felt a warmth in his chest that had nothing to do with the magical note. This was what real magic looked like - people coming together, working hard, all to help a friend in need.

A Day of Hope and Hard Work

Sunday dawned bright and clear as if even the weather was on their side. Jake was up before the sun, his mind buzzing with last-minute details. As he got ready, his hand brushed against his backpack, feeling the outline of the magical note inside. For a moment, he hesitated. Should he bring it, just in case?

In the end, he left it at home. Today wasn't about easy solutions or magical fixes. It was about community, hard work, and the power of friendship.

The day was a whirlwind of activity. Jake ran from one task to another, barely stopping to catch his breath. He manned the car wash, helped at the bake sale, and even performed a clumsy but enthusiastic dance routine in the talent show.

Throughout it all, he kept an eye on Alex. His friend was working just as hard, a look of determination on his face. But Jake could also see the worry there, the fear that it might not be enough despite all their efforts.

The Final Tally

As the sun began to set, the festivities wound down. Exhausted but exhilarated, Jake, Alex, their friends, and the adult volunteers gathered to count the money they'd raised.

Jake held his breath as the final numbers were tallied. He thought again of the magical note, safely tucked away in his room. If they fell short, could he find a way to use it without raising suspicion?

But as the final total was announced, Jake realised he needn't have worried. They'd done it. Through the combined efforts of the entire neighbourhood, they'd raised not just the $2000 Alex's family needed but an additional $500 to help them get back on their feet.

The room erupted in cheers. Jake turned to Alex, seeing tears in his friend's eyes. But this time, they were tears of joy and relief.

The Power of Community

As the crowd dispersed and they began cleaning up, Jake and Alex found a quiet moment to talk.

"I can't believe we did it," Alex said, his voice filled with awe. "Jake, I don't know how to thank you. You organised all of this..."

Jake shook his head. "We all did this, Alex. The whole neighbourhood. That's what friends and community are for."

As he said the words, Jake realised how true they were. He thought about the magical note again, about how easy it would have been to use it. But would that have been the right solution?

This experience had taught him something valuable. Sometimes, the best solutions weren't the easiest ones. Sometimes, the real magic came from hard work, people coming together, facing challenges head-on rather than looking for quick fixes.

A Lesson Learned

That night, as Jake lay in bed, exhausted but happy, he reflected on the weekend's events. He'd been tempted, so tempted, to use the magical note to solve Alex's problem. It would have been quick, easy, and simple.

But by resisting that temptation, by rallying their friends and community instead, they'd achieved something far greater than just raising money. They'd shown Alex's family that they weren't alone, that they had a whole neighbourhood standing behind them. They'd created memories and strengthened bonds that would last far longer than any magical money ever could.

Jake realised that the note, for all its power, had limitations. It could create money, yes, but it couldn't create the warmth of friendship, the strength of community, or the satisfaction of overcoming a challenge through hard work and determination.

As he drifted off to sleep, Jake felt a new appreciation for the lessons the magical note was teaching him. It wasn't just about having the power to help others - it was about understanding the best way to help, even when that way wasn't the easiest.

Moving Forward

The next morning, Jake met Alex on the way to school. His friend looked different - lighter, somehow, as if a great weight had been lifted from his shoulders.

"My parents talked to the landlord last night," Alex said, a smile spreading across his face. "We're not getting evicted. And you know what else? The community centre offered my dad a job as a maintenance worker. Things are looking up."

Jake felt a surge of happiness for his friend. "That's fantastic, Alex! I'm so glad it all worked out."

As they walked, Alex turned to Jake with a serious expression. "You know, when I called you on Saturday, I was so scared. I didn't know what to do, didn't think there was any way out. But you... you didn't just give me money or an easy fix. You showed me that we're not alone and have friends and neighbours who care about us. That's worth more than any amount of money."

Jake nodded, thinking about the magical note. "Sometimes the best solutions are the ones we work for," he said. "And sometimes, the real magic is in the people around us."

As they approached the school, Jake felt a renewed sense of purpose. The magical note was a powerful tool, but this experience had shown him that there was often more than one way to solve a problem.

Sometimes, the best solution wasn't the quickest or easiest one, but the one that brought people together and created lasting change.

He knew that there would be more challenges ahead and more opportunities to use the note's power. But now, he felt better equipped to make the right choices. The magic wasn't just in the note - it was in the wisdom to know when to use it and when to rely on the strength of friendship and community instead.

As they entered the school grounds, Jake saw their friends waiting for them, all smiling proudly. He realised that this adventure had not only helped Alex's family but had also strengthened their entire group of friends. They had faced a significant challenge together and had come out stronger on the other side.

Jake couldn't help but wonder what other lessons the magical note had in store for him. But whatever came next, he felt ready to face it, armed with the knowledge and experiences he'd gained. The journey was far from over, and Jake was eager to see where it would lead next.

Chapter 5

The Bully's Challenge

Jake's heart race as he stepped into the school courtyard, his hand instinctively reaching for the magical note tucked safely in his pocket. The past few weeks had been a whirlwind of excitement and moral dilemmas, but nothing could have prepared him for what awaited him today.

A familiar sense of dread washed over him as he approached his usual spot by the oak tree. There, leaning against the trunk with a smug grin, stood Zack Thompson – the school's notorious bully. Jake's stomach churned as he remembered their last encounter, which had left him with a bruised ego and a missing lunch.

The Confrontation

"Well, well, well," Zack drawled, pushing himself off the tree and sauntering towards Jake. "If it isn't little Jake the Snake. Got any lunch money for me today?"

You might think that having a magical note that could solve all his problems would make Jake feel invincible. But at that moment, as Zack towered over him, Jake felt smaller than ever. The note's weight in his pocket seemed to grow heavier, almost as if it reminded him of its presence.

"I... I don't have any money, Zack," Jake stammered, his mind racing. He could feel the note's warmth against his leg, practically begging to be used. But something held him back. Was it fear? Or was it something else?"

Zack's eyes narrowed dangerously. "Wrong answer, Snake. I know you've been holding out on me. I've seen you helping people around town and buying stuff. You've got money somewhere, and I want it."

As Zack reached out to grab Jake's collar, time seemed to slow down. At that moment, Jake had a choice to make. He could use the note to make Zack disappear, to teach him a lesson he'd never forget. It would be so easy, wouldn't it? Just a thought and all his problems would vanish.

But as his fingers brushed against the note in his pocket, Jake hesitated. The lessons he'd learned over the past few weeks came flooding back to him. The homeless man's grateful smile, his best friend's relief, the joy on people's faces at the community fair. Was this really how he wanted to use the note's power?

The Inner Struggle

I want you to imagine yourself in Jake's shoes for a moment. You're faced with someone who's been tormenting you for months, maybe even years. You have the power to make it all stop with just a thought. What would you do?

It's not an easy decision, is it? The temptation to use power for personal gain or revenge is something we all struggle with, whether we have a magical note or not. It's in these moments that our true character is revealed.

For Jake, this was more than just a confrontation with a bully. It was a test of everything he'd learned, of the person he was becoming. As Zack's grip tightened on his collar, Jake made his decision.

"Let go of me, Zack," he said, his voice steadier than he felt. "I don't have any money for you, and even if I did, I wouldn't give it to you."

Zack's eyes widened in surprise, then narrowed in anger. "You've got some nerve, Snake. Maybe I need to teach you a lesson."

As Zack pulled back his fist, Jake closed his eyes, bracing for the impact. But it never came.

An Unexpected Ally

"That's enough, Zack," a voice called out. Jake's eyes flew open to see Ms. Rodriguez, the school counsellor, striding towards them. "Let him go. Now."

Zack released Jake's collar, taking a step back. "We were just talking, Ms. R. No big deal."

Ms. Rodriguez raised an eyebrow. "Is that so? Well, I think you and I need to have a little chat in my office. Now."

As Zack slouched away, muttering under his breath, Ms. Rodriguez turned to Jake. "Are you alright, Jake?"

Jake nodded, still a bit shaken. "I'm fine, Ms. Rodriguez. Thank you."

She smiled warmly. "You know, Jake, I saw what happened. You stood up to him, even when you were scared. That takes real courage."

Jake felt a warmth spread through his chest that had nothing to do with the magical note. "I... I just knew it wasn't right to give in to him,"

Ms. Rodriguez nodded approvingly. "That's a valuable lesson, Jake. Sometimes, the right thing to do is also the hardest thing to do. But it's those choices that shape who we are."

As Ms. Rodriguez walked away, Jake's hand once again found the note in his pocket. But this time, instead of temptation, he felt a sense of pride. He had faced a challenge without relying on the note's power, and he had come out stronger for it.

The Aftermath

The rest of the day passed in a blur for Jake. His classmates, who had witnessed the confrontation, looked at him with newfound respect. Even Zack, when he returned from his meeting with Ms. Rodriguez, seemed subdued, avoiding Jake's gaze.

As Jake walked home that afternoon, he couldn't help but reflect on what had happened. He had been so close to using the note, to taking the easy way out. But something had stopped him. Was it the lessons he'd learned from his previous experiences with the note? Or was it something deeper, a part of himself that he was only now discovering?

I want you to think about a time when you faced a difficult decision. Maybe it wasn't as dramatic as confronting a bully, but I'm sure you've had moments where you've been tempted to take the easy way out. What stopped you? What made you choose the harder, but ultimately more rewarding path?

For Jake, this experience was a turning point. He realised that the note, while powerful, wasn't the solution to all his problems. Sometimes, the strength he needed was already within him.

A New Perspective

That evening, as Jake sat at his desk, the homework spread out before him, he found his thoughts drifting back to Zack. For the first time, he began to wonder about the bully's life. What made Zack act the way he did? Was there something going on in his life that Jake didn't know about?

Jake remembered how Ms. Rodriguez had intervened, how she had spoken to Zack. She hadn't yelled or threatened punishment. Instead, she had offered to talk. Maybe, Jake thought, that was the key.

Maybe what Zack needed wasn't fear or retaliation, but understanding.

It was a strange thought, feeling empathy for someone who had caused him so much trouble. But as Jake rolled the idea around in his mind, it began to make more and more sense. After all, hadn't the magical note taught him about the power of kindness and understanding?

The Plan

As Jake got ready for bed that night, a plan began to form in his mind. He couldn't change Zack overnight, and he certainly couldn't use the note to magically make Zack a better person. But maybe, just maybe, he could make a difference in a smaller way.

He thought about what he knew about Zack. Despite his tough exterior, Jake had noticed that Zack always seemed to be alone. He never talked about friends or family, and he always ate lunch by himself.

An idea struck Jake. What if he invited Zack to join him and his friends for lunch tomorrow? It was a small gesture, but it could be a start. The thought of approaching Zack again made Jake's palms sweat, but he knew it was the right thing to do. As he drifted off to sleep, Jake's hand rested lightly on the magical note under his pillow. For the first time since he'd found it, he felt like he truly understood its purpose. It wasn't about having the power to change the world in grand, sweeping gestures. It was about the small acts of kindness, the moments of courage, the choices we make every day to be better than we were yesterday.

The Next Day

The following morning, Jake walked into school with a mix of determination and nervousness. He spotted Zack at his locker, looking unusually subdued. Taking a deep breath, Jake approached him.

"Hey, Zack," he said, his voice only trembling slightly.

Zack looked up, surprise and wariness battling in his eyes. "What do you want, Snake?"

Jake swallowed hard. "I, uh, I was wondering if you wanted to join me and my friends for lunch today."

The look of shock on Zack's face would have been comical if Jake wasn't so nervous. "Is this some kind of joke?" Zack asked, his voice lacking its usual aggression.

Jake shook his head. "No joke. Just... an invitation. If you want."

For a long moment, Zack just stared at him. Then, almost imperceptibly, he nodded. "Yeah... okay. Whatever."

As Jake walked away, his heart pounding with a mixture of relief and excitement, he couldn't help but smile. He had no idea how lunch would go, or if this small act would make any difference in the long run. But he knew he had made the right choice.

The Ripple Effect

Over the next few weeks, Jake watched in amazement as his small act of kindness began to create ripples throughout the school. Zack, while still rough around the edges, began to soften. He stopped bullying other students and even started to make friends of his own.

Other students, inspired by Jake's example, began reaching out to those who were usually left out or picked on. The atmosphere in the school began to change, becoming more inclusive and supportive.

Jake couldn't help but wonder if this was the true magic of the note. Not in its ability to grant wishes or create money out of thin air, but in the way it had opened his eyes to the power of kindness and empathy.

A Moment of Reflection

One afternoon, as Jake sat under the oak tree where his confrontation with Zack had taken place, he pulled out the magical note. Its soft glow seemed different now, warmer somehow. As he traced its edges with his finger, he thought about how far he had come since first finding it.

He had learned about generosity from the homeless man, about self-control in the toy store, about loyalty with his best friend. But this latest lesson, about the power of empathy and the courage to do what's right even when it's hard, felt like the most important one yet.

Jake realised that the note hadn't just been giving him the power to help others. It had been teaching him, guiding him, helping him grow into the person he was meant to be.

As the sun began to set, casting long shadows across the schoolyard, Jake carefully tucked the note back into his pocket. He didn't know what challenges tomorrow would bring, but he felt ready to face them. Not because he had a magical note, but because of what that note had taught him about himself.

The Conversation

A few days later, Jake found himself face to face with Zack again. But this time, there was no tension, no fear. They were simply two boys talking after school.

"I don't get it, Jake," Zack said, his brow furrowed in confusion. "Why did you invite me to lunch that day? After everything I did to you?"

Jake thought carefully before answering. "I guess... I realised that everyone deserves a chance. And maybe what you needed wasn't someone to fight back, but someone to reach out."

Zack was quiet for a long moment. "You know," he said finally, "no one's ever done anything like that for me before. It... it meant a lot."

As they parted ways, Jake felt a warmth in his chest that had nothing to do with the magical note. He had made a difference, not through grand gestures or magical intervention, but through a simple act of kindness.

The Lesson Learned

That night, as Jake lay in bed, he reflected on everything that had happened. He thought about the bully's challenge, the decision he had made, and the unexpected outcomes that had followed.

He realised that the true magic wasn't in the note at all. It was in the choices we make every day, in the way we treat others, in the courage to do what's right even when it's difficult.

As he drifted off to sleep, Jake smiled to himself. He didn't know what new challenges tomorrow would bring, but he felt ready to face them. Not because he had a magical note in his pocket, but because he had learned the most important lesson of all: the real magic was inside him all along.

Looking Ahead

As Jake closed his eyes, his mind couldn't help but wonder about what might come next. The magical note had already led him on so many adventures, taught him so many lessons. What else did it have in store for him?

He thought about the mysterious stranger he had glimpsed around town a few times. The one who seemed to appear and disappear at will, who always seemed to be watching Jake with a knowing smile. Who was he? Did he know about the note?

These questions swirled in Jake's mind as he fell asleep, the magical note glowing softly under his pillow. Little did he know that his greatest adventure was yet to come, and that the lessons he had learned would soon be put to the ultimate test.

But that, dear reader, is a story for another chapter.

Chapter 6

The Mysterious Stranger

Jake's journey with the magical note had been nothing short of extraordinary. From helping a homeless man to resisting the temptations of a toy store, supporting his best friend, and facing a school bully, he had learned valuable lessons about empathy, self-control, loyalty, and conflict resolution. Little did he know that his adventure was about to take an even more intriguing turn.

As Jake walked home from school one crisp autumn afternoon, the weight of the magical note in his pocket seemed heavier than usual. He couldn't shake the feeling that something significant was about to happen. The leaves crunched beneath his feet, and a cool breeze rustled through the trees, sending a shiver down his spine.

An Unexpected Encounter

Just as Jake turned the corner onto his street, he noticed a figure standing beneath a flickering streetlight. The person seemed to appear out of nowhere, and there was something about them that made Jake's heart race. As he approached, he realised it was an elderly man with a long, silver beard and piercing blue eyes that seemed to look right through him.

"Hello, young Jake," the man said, his voice warm and gravelly. "I've been waiting for you."

Jake froze in his tracks, his hand instinctively moving to his pocket where the magical note lay hidden. "How do you know my name?" he asked, trying to keep his voice steady.

The old man smiled, the wrinkles around his eyes deepening. "I know many things, Jake. Including the fact that you carry something very special in your pocket."

Jake's eyes widened. Could this stranger really know about the magical note? He had been so careful to keep it a secret. "I... I don't know what you're talking about," he stammered, taking a step back.

The Revelation

The old man chuckled softly. "There's no need to be afraid, Jake. I'm here to help you understand the power you've been entrusted with."

Jake's curiosity got the better of him. "You know about the note? Who are you?"

"My name is Elias," the man replied, "and I've been watching over that note for a very long time. It's a responsibility that has been passed down through generations, and now it has found its way to you."

Jake's mind was reeling. He had so many questions, but he didn't know where to start. "But why me? I'm just a regular kid."

Elias's eyes twinkled. "Are you, Jake? The note doesn't choose just anyone. It seeks out those with a pure heart and the potential to make a real difference in the world."

The Note's Origin

As the sun began to set, casting long shadows across the street, Elias gestured to a nearby bench. "Shall we sit? There's much to discuss."

Jake nodded, following the old man to the bench. As they sat down, Elias began to speak, his voice taking on a storyteller's cadence.

"The note you carry, Jake, is no ordinary piece of currency. It was created centuries ago by a powerful alchemist who sought to test humanity's capacity for kindness and wisdom. The alchemist imbued the note with magical properties, allowing it to multiply and change its value based on the intentions of its holder."

Jake listened, fascinated. "So that's why it seems to always have the right amount when I need to help someone!"

Elias nodded. "Exactly. But the note's power goes beyond mere multiplication. It has the ability to reveal the true nature of those who possess it. In the right hands, it can be a force for tremendous good. In the wrong hands, it can lead to greed and destruction."

The Test of Character

Jake's brow furrowed as he considered Elias's words. "Is that why I've been facing all these challenges? To test my character?"

"You're a perceptive young man, Jake," Elias said with approval. "Yes, each situation you've encountered has been a test. The homeless man tested your empathy, the toy stores your self-control, your friend's problem tested your loyalty, and the bully tested your ability to resolve conflicts peacefully."

Jake felt a swell of pride at having passed these tests, but also a twinge of uncertainty. "But what if I make a mistake? What if I use the note for the wrong reasons?"

Elias placed a comforting hand on Jake's shoulder. "That's the beauty of it, Jake. The note doesn't expect perfection. It's about learning and growing. Every decision you make, every challenge you face, shapes who you are and how you use the note's power."

The Greater Purpose

As night fell and the streetlights flickered to life, Jake's mind was buzzing with new information. But one question still nagged him. "Elias, what's the ultimate purpose of the note? Why does it exist?"

The old man's expression grew serious. "The note, Jake, is a tool for change. In the right hands, it has the power to make the world a better place, one act of kindness at a time. But its true potential is only realised when its holder understands the value of wisdom, compassion, and selflessness."

Jake nodded slowly, beginning to understand. "So, it's not just about helping people with money, is it? It's about learning how to make the right choices and use resources wisely."

"Precisely," Elias said, his eyes twinkling with pride. "You're beginning to see the bigger picture, Jake. The note is as much about personal growth as it is about helping others."

The Road Ahead

As their conversation drew to a close, Jake felt both excited and overwhelmed by the responsibility he now knew he carried. "What happens now, Elias? Will I see you again?"

The old man stood up, his silver beard glowing softly in the moonlight. "Your journey is far from over, Jake. There will be more challenges ahead, each one designed to test your growing wisdom and compassion. As for me, I'll be watching over you, but this is your path to walk."

Jake stood up too, feeling a new sense of purpose. "I'll do my best, Elias. I promise."

Elias smiled warmly. "I know you will, Jake. Remember, the true magic doesn't lie in the note, itself, but in the choices you make and the person you become."

With those parting words, Elias turned and walked away, seeming to fade into the shadows. Jake watched him go, his mind swirling with all he had learned.

A New Perspective

As Jake made his way home, the magical note in his pocket felt different somehow. It was no longer just a mysterious object, but a symbol of the responsibility he carried and the potential for growth and change.

He thought about all the people he had helped so far and the lessons he had learned. Each experience had shaped him, teaching him valuable lessons about empathy, self-control, loyalty, and problem-solving. Now, armed with the knowledge Elias had shared, Jake felt ready to face whatever challenges lay ahead.

The encounter with the mysterious stranger had deepened the mystery of the magical note, but it had also given Jake a clearer sense of purpose. He realised that his journey was about more than just helping individuals; it was about learning to make wise decisions that could have a positive impact on the world around him.

As he reached his front door, Jake paused for a moment, looking up at the star-filled sky. He made a silent promise to himself and to Elias: he would use the note's power responsibly, continue to learn and grow, and strive to make a real difference in the world.

Little did Jake know that his greatest challenges and most important lessons were still to come. The magical note had more in store for him, and the wisdom he had gained from Elias would soon be put to the test in ways he couldn't imagine.

With a deep breath, Jake stepped into his house, ready to face whatever tomorrow might bring. The magical note hummed softly in his pocket, a reminder of the extraordinary journey he was on and the potential for good that lay within his grasp.

Chapter 7

The Community Fair

As Jake approached the bustling community fair, the magical note in his pocket seemed to pulse with energy. The air was filled with the sweet scent of cotton candy and the excited chatter of families enjoying the festivities. Jake couldn't help but smile, feeling a sense of anticipation for what the day might bring.

A New Perspective

You know that feeling when you're surrounded by joy and laughter? That's exactly how Jake felt as he stepped into the fairgrounds. The colourful banners, the cheerful music, and the smiling faces all around him painted a picture of pure happiness. But as he walked further into the fair, Jake began to notice something he hadn't seen before.

Amidst the sea of joyful faces, there were a few that stood out - not for their happiness, but for their worry and concern. It was as if the magical note had sharpened Jake's senses, allowing him to see beyond the surface of the festive atmosphere.

I remember a time when I attended a similar fair as a child. At first, all I could see were the exciting rides and games. But as the day went on, I started to notice the hard work of the volunteers, the struggles of some families to afford the attractions, and the lonely elderly visitors sitting on benches. It was a moment of awakening, much like what Jake was experiencing now.

The First Act of Kindness

As Jake wandered through the fair, he came across a small booth run by the local animal shelter. A kind- looking woman was desperately trying to encourage people to adopt the adorable puppies and kittens in cages beside her. Despite her efforts, most people walked by without a second glance.

Jake felt a tug in his heart. He remembered the homeless man he had helped earlier and how good it had felt to make a difference. Without hesitation, he approached the booth.

"Hi there," Jake said, smiling at the woman, "Is there anything I can do to help?"

The woman's eyes lit up. "Oh, that's so kind of you to offer! We're trying to raise money for the shelter and find homes for these little ones. But it's been a slow day."

Jake nodded, an idea forming in his mind. He reached into his pocket and felt the warmth of the magical note. Carefully, he pulled it out and handed it to the woman.

"I'd like to make a donation," he said.

The woman's eyes widened as she looked at the note. "Oh my! This is so generous. Thank you!"

As she put the note in the donation box, Jake watched in amazement as it seemed to multiply. Suddenly, the box was overflowing with donations.

The woman gasped. "I can't believe it! Look at all these donations. This will help so many animals!"

Jake felt a warmth spread through his chest. He had used the note's power to help, and the result was immediate and impactful.

The Ripple Effect

Word of the animal shelter's sudden influx of donations spread quickly through the fair. People began to gather around the booth, curious about the commotion. As they learned about the shelter's mission, many were inspired to make their own donations or consider adopting a pet.

Jake watched from a distance, marvelling at how one act of kindness could create such a positive ripple effect. It reminded me of a quote I once heard: "No act of kindness, no matter how small, is ever wasted." Jake saw this wisdom come to life before his very eyes.

The Struggling Artist

As Jake continued his journey through the fair, he came across a young artist sitting dejectedly by her booth. Her paintings were beautiful - vibrant landscapes and portraits that seemed to come alive on the canvas. Yet, her booth was empty of customers.

Jake approached her, drawn by both her talent and her obvious distress. "These are amazing," he said, gesturing to the paintings.

The artist looked up, a glimmer of hope in her eyes. "Thank you," she replied. "But I haven't sold a single one today. I was hoping to make enough to cover my rent this month."

Jake felt that familiar tug in his heart. He reached for the magical note once again, this time using it to purchase one of her paintings. As he handed over the note, he watched in awe as more customers suddenly appeared, eager to buy the artist's work.

Within an hour, the artist's booth was buzzing with activity. Every painting was sold, and she was taking commissions for future works. The joy and relief on her face were palpable.

"I don't know how to thank you," she said to Jake, tears of happiness in her eyes. "You've changed everything for me today."

Jake smiled, feeling a sense of fulfilment wash over him. He was beginning to understand the true power of the magical note — it wasn't just about creating money but about creating opportunities for kindness and positive change.

The Elderly Couple

As the day wore on, Jake found himself drawn to an elderly couple sitting on a bench near the Ferris wheel. They were watching the families and children with a wistful look in their eyes.

Jake approached them, feeling compelled to reach out. "Hi there," he said. "Are you enjoying the fair?"

The old man smiled sadly. "Oh, we love seeing all the happiness around us. But at our age, we can't really participate in much. We just come to remember the good old days when we used to bring our kids here."

His wife nodded in agreement. "We used to love the Ferris wheel," she added. "But now, with Arthur's bad knee and my dizzy spells, we can't risk it."

Jake felt a lump in his throat. He looked at the magical note in his hand and then at the Ferris wheel. An idea struck him.

"What if I told you there was a way you could enjoy the Ferris wheel again?" he asked.

The couple looked at him curiously as Jake approached the Ferris wheel operator. He handed over the magical note, whispering his request. The operator's eyes widened, and he nodded enthusiastically.

A few minutes later, the Ferris wheel came to a stop. The operator approached the elderly couple with a wheelchair ramp and invited them for a special, slow-paced ride.

The joy on their faces as they were carefully helped onto the Ferris wheel was indescribable. Jake watched as they slowly ascended, their hands clasped together, reliving a cherished memory.

When they returned to the ground, both had tears in their eyes. "Young man," the old woman said, grasping Jake's hand. "You've given us a priceless gift today. Thank you."

The Lost Child

As the afternoon progressed, Jake noticed a commotion near the cotton candy stand. A young mother was frantically searching for her child, tears streaming down her face.

"Tommy!" she called out, her voice breaking with fear. "Has anyone seen my Tommy?"

Jake felt his heart race. He knew he had to help. He approached the distraught mother, offering his assistance. Together, they began searching the fairgrounds, calling out for Tommy.

As they searched, Jake felt the magical note grow warm in his pocket. He pulled it out, and to his amazement, it seemed to be guiding him. Following its lead, Jake and the mother made their way to the petting zoo at the far end of the fair.

There, hidden behind a large hay bale, they found Tommy. The little boy had wandered off, fascinated by the animals and had fallen asleep in the warm afternoon sun.

The mother's cry of relief as she scooped up her son was heart-wrenching. She turned to Jake, gratitude shining in her eyes. "How can I ever thank you?" she asked.

Jake shook his head, smiling. "Seeing Tommy safe is all the thanks I need," he replied.

As they walked back to the main area of the fair, Jake noticed something extraordinary. The magical note had multiplied again, this time into several smaller notes. He discreetly handed them to the mother.

"Here," he said, "To make sure Tommy has a special day at the fair."

The mother's eyes widened as she looked at the money in her hand. "This is too much," she protested. Jake just smiled. "Everyone deserves a little magic at the fair," he said.

The Food Bank Booth

As the day began to wind down, Jake found himself drawn to a small, unassuming booth near the exit. It was for the local food bank, and a tired-looking volunteer was packing up, looking disappointed.

"Not a good day?" Jake asked, approaching the booth.

The volunteer sighed. "Not really. People come to the fair to have fun, not to think about hunger in the community. We barely got any donations."

Jake felt a familiar stirring in his heart. He reached for the magical note one last time, feeling its warmth in his hand. As he placed it in the donation box, he watched in awe as it multiplied, filling the box to the brim.

The volunteer's jaw dropped. "I can't believe it," she whispered. "This... this will feed so many families. Thank you!"

Jake smiled, feeling a sense of completion. He had used the note's power to spread joy and help throughout the day, and now, as the fair was ending, he was ensuring that its magic would continue to benefit the community long after the rides were dismantled and the booths packed away.

The Lesson Learned

As Jake left the fairgrounds, the setting sun painting the sky in vibrant oranges and pinks, he felt a profound sense of satisfaction. The magical note had given him the power to help others in ways he never thought possible.

But more than that, Jake realised that the true magic wasn't in the note itself. It was in the act of giving, of spreading kindness and joy. The note had simply been a tool - the real power had been in Jake's choices and actions.

I remember feeling a similar realisation after volunteering at a local charity event. The joy of helping others, of making a positive difference in someone's life, was a kind of magic all its own. It's a feeling that stays with you long after the event is over.

As Jake walked home, he thought about all the people he had helped that day - the animal shelter volunteer, the struggling artist, the elderly couple, the lost child and his mother, and the food bank volunteer. Each act of kindness had created a ripple effect, touching not just the immediate recipients but spreading out to affect others in ways Jake couldn't even imagine.

He realised that you don't need a magical note to make a difference. Every day, we all have opportunities to help others, to spread kindness, to make the world a little bit better. Sometimes it's a grand gesture, but more often, it's the small acts of kindness that truly change lives.

Jake felt changed by his experience at the community fair. He had learned the joy of selfless giving and the power of community spirit. As he reached home, he knew that tomorrow would bring new opportunities to spread kindness and make a difference, magical note or not.

And as he drifted off to sleep that night, Jake couldn't help but wonder what new adventures and lessons the magical note had in store for him. Little did he know his greatest challenge was yet to come - a test that would force him to confront his values and question the true meaning of happiness.

Chapter 8

The Ultimate Temptation

As Jake stepped out of his house that morning, the magical note tucked safely in his pocket, he couldn't shake the feeling that something extraordinary was about to happen. The air felt charged with anticipation, and the note seemed to pulse with an energy he had never felt before.

Little did Jake know that today would bring his greatest challenge yet – a test that would push him to the very limits of his newfound wisdom and force him to confront the true meaning of happiness.

An Unexpected Encounter

Jake was walking to school, his mind preoccupied with thoughts about the upcoming math test, when a sleek black limousine pulled up beside him. The tinted window rolled down, revealing a man in an impeccable suit, his silver hair slicked back and a diamond-encrusted watch glinting on his wrist.

"Hello, young man," the stranger said, his voice smooth as silk. "I couldn't help but notice something special about you. Would you mind if we had a little chat?"

Jake hesitated. He had always been taught not to talk to strangers, but there was something compelling about this man. Plus, the magical note in his pocket seemed to hum with excitement, as if urging him forward.

"It's alright," the man said, sensing Jake's hesitation. "I'm Mr. Goldstein, and I have a proposition that might interest you."

Curiosity got the better of Jake, and he found himself nodding. Mr. Goldstein opened the car door, and Jake slid into the plush leather seats, marvelling at the luxury surrounding him.

The Offer of a Lifetime

As the limousine glided through the streets, Mr. Goldstein turned to Jake with a gleam in his eye. "I'll get straight to the point, Jake. I know about your special... ability."

Jake's heart skipped a beat. How could this stranger know about the magical note?

Mr. Goldstein chuckled at Jake's shocked expression. "Don't worry, my boy. I'm not here to take it away from you. In fact, I'm here to offer you an opportunity of a lifetime."

He paused for effect before continuing, "What if I told you that I could make you incredibly wealthy? Not just rich, Jake, but wealthy beyond your wildest dreams."

Jake's mind reeled. He thought about all the good he could do with that kind of money. He could help his parents pay off their mortgage, fund his sister's college education, and donate to countless charities.

"How?" Jake asked, his voice barely above a whisper.

Mr. Goldstein leaned in closer. "It's simple. You have a gift, Jake. A gift that can create money out of thin air. All you need to do is use it... a lot. Create as much money as you can, and I'll show you how to invest it, how to make it grow. In no time, you'll be one of the richest people in the world."

The Weight of Temptation

As Mr. Goldstein spoke, Jake felt the weight of the magical note in his pocket grow heavier. It was as if the note itself was urging him to consider the offer carefully.

Jake's mind raced with possibilities. He imagined himself living in a mansion, driving fancy cars, and never having to worry about money again. He could buy anything he wanted, go anywhere he desired. The world would be at his fingertips.

But then, unbidden, memories of his recent adventures flashed through his mind. He remembered the homeless man he had helped, the joy on his friend's face when he solved her problem, and the sense of

He felt accomplishment after resolving the conflict with the bully without resorting to revenge. "What's the catch?" Jake asked, suddenly wary.

Mr. Goldstein's smile widened. "Clever boy. The catch, as you put it, is simple. You'll need to focus all your energy on creating money and growing your wealth. No more helping random strangers or solving petty problems. Your gift is too valuable for that. You'll need to think big, Jake. World-changing big."

The Inner Struggle

As the limousine continued its journey, Jake felt torn. On one hand, the prospect of unlimited wealth was intoxicating. He could do so much good with that kind of money, couldn't he? He could fund research to cure diseases, build schools in underprivileged areas, and support environmental conservation efforts on a massive scale.

But on the other hand, something felt... off. The magical note had taught him so much about the joy of helping others directly, about the value of personal connections and the importance of empathy. Could he really give all that up?

Jake closed his eyes, trying to quiet the conflicting voices in his head. He thought about his parents and how hard they worked to provide for the family. He remembered his mother's words: "Money isn't everything, Jake. True happiness comes from within."

He thought about the mysterious stranger who had hinted at the note's true purpose. Was this what he meant? Was this the ultimate test?

A Moment of Clarity

As Jake wrestled with his decision, he felt the magical note grow warm in his pocket. Suddenly, a moment of clarity washed over him like a cool breeze on a hot summer day.

He realised that the joy he had experienced over the past few weeks hadn't come from the money itself, but from the act of helping others. It wasn't about the amount of money he could create, but about the direct impact he could have on people's lives.

Jake turned to Mr. Goldstein, his decision made. "Thank you for the offer, Mr. Goldstein, but I have to decline."

The man's smooth facade cracked for a moment, revealing a flash of disappointment and... was that respect?

"Are you sure, Jake? This is a once-in-a-lifetime opportunity. You could have everything you've ever wanted."

Jake smiled, feeling a sense of peace settle over him. "I already have everything I need, Mr. Goldstein. And I've learned that true happiness doesn't come from having everything you want, but from appreciating what you have and helping others."

The True Test

As Jake spoke these words, the magical note in his pocket began to glow brightly, its warmth spreading through his entire body. In that moment, Jake understood that this had been the true test all along.

The note wasn't just about creating money; it was about understanding the true value of wealth and happiness. It was about learning to make the right choices, even when faced with overwhelming temptation.

Mr. Goldstein's expression softened, and for a moment, Jake saw a glimmer of something else in the man's eyes – a mixture of pride and perhaps a touch of envy.

"You've made a wise choice, Jake," Mr. Goldstein said, his voice tinged with respect. "Not many would have the strength to turn down such an offer. You've passed a test that many adults fail."

As the limousine pulled up to Jake's school, Mr. Goldstein handed him a business card. "If you ever change your mind, or if you need any help in the future, don't hesitate to call."

Jake took the card, knowing he would never use it, but appreciating the gesture, nonetheless.

A New Understanding

As Jake stepped out of the limousine and watched it drive away, he felt as though a weight had been lifted from his shoulders. The magical note in his pocket felt lighter, almost playful, as if it was congratulating him on his choice.

He realised that the true power of the note wasn't in its ability to create money, but in its capacity to teach valuable life lessons. It had shown him the importance of empathy, generosity, self-control, loyalty, and now, the true meaning of wealth and happiness.

Jake walked into school that day with a spring in his step and a new understanding of his journey with the magical note. He knew that whatever challenges lay ahead, he was now better equipped to face them with wisdom and compassion.

As he sat down for his math test, Jake couldn't help but smile. He had faced the ultimate temptation and emerged stronger for it. Whatever the magical note had in store for him next, he was ready.

The Ripple Effect

In the days that followed, Jake noticed a change in himself. He felt more confident, more at peace with who he was and the choices he made. His friends and family noticed it too, commenting on his newfound maturity and wisdom.

Jake continued to use the magical note to help others, but now he did so with a deeper understanding of its purpose. He realised that every act of kindness, no matter how small, created a ripple effect that could change the world in ways he couldn't even imagine.

He thought about Mr. Goldstein's offer and how different his life would be if he had accepted it. Sure, he would have been wealthy beyond measure, but at what cost? He would have lost the joy of personal connections, the satisfaction of solving problems with his own ingenuity, and the warmth that came from helping others directly.

Lessons Learned

As Jake reflected on his journey so far, he identified several key lessons he had learned:

1. True wealth isn't measured in dollars and cents, but in the richness of experiences and relationships.

2. Happiness comes from within and is often found in the act of helping others.

3. The greatest temptations often come disguised as opportunities.

4. It's important to stay true to your values, even when faced with life-changing decisions.

5. Sometimes, saying no to something good opens the door to something even better.

These lessons had transformed Jake from a typical kid into someone who understood the deeper truths of life and happiness. He felt grateful for the magical note and the journey it had taken him on.

Looking Ahead

As Jake lay in bed that night, the magical note tucked safely under his pillow, he couldn't help but wonder what other adventures and lessons awaited him. He had faced his greatest temptation and emerged stronger, but he had a feeling that his journey with the magical note was far from over.

What other tests would he face? What other truths would he uncover? And most importantly, how would these experiences shape him and his understanding of the world?

With these thoughts swirling in his mind, Jake drifted off to sleep, eager to see what tomorrow would bring. Little did he know that the greatest revelation about the magical note was yet to come, and it would change everything he thought he knew about its purpose and his role in its story.

As the moon cast a soft glow through his bedroom window, the magical note pulsed with a gentle light, as if acknowledging Jake's growth and preparing him for the final leg of his extraordinary journey.

The Power of Choice

The next morning, as Jake got ready for school, he found himself thinking about the power of choice. He realised that every decision he made, no matter how small, had the potential to shape his future and impact those around him.

He thought about all the choices he had made since finding the magical note:

- Choosing to help the homeless man instead of keeping the money for himself

- Deciding not to buy everything he wanted at the toy store

- Finding a way to help his friend without revealing the note's secret

- Resolving the conflict with the bully without resorting to revenge

- And now, turning down the opportunity to become incredibly wealthy

Each of these choices had taught him something valuable and had contributed to his personal growth. Jake understood that life was a series of choices, and it was these decisions that defined who he was as a person.

A New Perspective on Wealth

As Jake walked to school, he saw his neighbourhood with new eyes. He noticed the small acts of kindness between neighbours, the joy of children playing in the park, and the sense of community that permeated the air. He realised that these things, which couldn't be bought with any amount of money, were the true wealth of his community.

He thought about Mr. Goldstein and wondered if the man, for all his material wealth, had ever experienced the simple joy of helping a stranger or the warmth of a friend's gratitude. Jake felt a twinge of sadness for the man, understanding now that true richness came from connections and experiences, not from a bank account balance.

The Responsibility of Power

As the day progressed, Jake found himself pondering the responsibility that came with the magical note's power. He realised that having the ability to create money at will was an enormous responsibility, one that required wisdom and restraint.

He thought about how easy it would have been to accept Mr. Goldstein's offer, to use the note's power for personal gain. But he also understood that with great power comes great responsibility. The note had chosen him for a reason, and it was his duty to use its power wisely and for the greater good.

Jake made a silent promise to himself and to the magical note that he would always strive to make choices that aligned with his values and benefited others, not just himself.

The Unseen Impact

During lunch, Jake overheard a conversation between two teachers. They were discussing a recent anonymous donation to the school that would fund new books for the library and musical instruments for the band.

With a start, Jake realised that this was the result of one of his earlier uses of the magical note. He had created some extra money and donated it to the school, never expecting to hear about it again.

Listening to the teachers' excitement and imagining the impact this donation would have on his fellow students, Jake felt a warm glow of satisfaction. He realised that sometimes the best acts of kindness were the ones where you never saw the direct impact. The magical note was teaching him about the joy of anonymous giving and the far-reaching effects of generosity.

A Test of Character

As the final bell rang and Jake prepared to head home, he was approached by his math teacher, Mr. Thompson. The teacher looked troubled as he asked Jake to stay back for a moment.

"Jake, I noticed something unusual during the test yesterday," Mr. Thompson began. "Your answers to the bonus question were identical to those of another student. I need to ask... did you cheat?"

Jake felt his heart race. He knew he hadn't cheated, but how could he explain the similarity? Then he remembered - he had used the magical note to help his struggling classmate understand the concept just before the test. They must have solved the problem the same way.

For a moment, Jake was tempted to use the note to create a distraction or even alter Mr. Thompson's memory. It would be so easy to avoid this uncomfortable situation. But as his hand brushed against the note in his pocket, he knew what he had to do.

Taking a deep breath, Jake looked his teacher in the eye. "I didn't cheat, Mr. Thompson. I helped my classmate understand the concept before the test. We must have solved it the same way. I'm sorry if it looked suspicious."

Mr. Thompson studied Jake's face for a moment before his expression softened. "Thank you for your honesty, Jake. I appreciate you telling me the truth. In the future, perhaps it's best to let your classmates work things out on their own before a test."

As Jake left the classroom, he felt a mixture of relief and pride. He had faced another test - not of math, but of character - and had chosen honesty over an easy escape.

The Bigger Picture

That evening, as Jake sat in his room, turning the magical note over in his hands, he found himself thinking about the bigger picture. What was the true purpose of this extraordinary gift he had been given?

It wasn't just about creating money or even about helping people at the moment. It was about learning, growing, and understanding the complex web of cause and effect that governed the world.

Every choice he made, every person he helped, created ripples that spread out in ways he couldn't always see or understand. The magical note was teaching him to think beyond the immediate, to consider the long-term consequences of his actions.

Jake realised that the journey he was on was shaping him into the person he was meant to become. Each challenge, each temptation, each moment of clarity was a step on this path of personal growth and understanding.

The Question of Worthiness

As Jake pondered these deep thoughts, a nagging question surfaced in his mind: Why him? Why had the magical note chosen him for this journey?

He didn't feel particularly special or wise. He was just a regular kid who had stumbled upon something extraordinary. Did he really deserve this power? Was he worthy of the responsibility it brought?

As if in response to his doubts, the magical note began to glow softly. Its warmth spread through Jake's hands, up his arms, and into his heart. In that moment, Jake understood that worthiness wasn't about being perfect or having all the answers. It was about being open to learning, being willing to make mistakes, and always striving to do what was right.

The note had chosen him not because he was already worthy, but because it saw the potential in him to grow, to learn, and to make a positive difference in the world.

The Road Ahead

As Jake prepared for bed that night, he felt a sense of anticipation for what was to come. He had faced his greatest temptation and had emerged stronger, wiser, and surer of himself than ever before.

But he also knew that his journey was far from over. There were still mysteries to unravel, lessons to learn, and challenges to face. What was the true secret of the magical note? What was its ultimate purpose? And how would his journey end?

As he drifted off to sleep, Jake felt ready for whatever lay ahead. He had learned to trust in himself, to value the right things, and to use his power responsibly. Whatever tests or revelations awaited him, he would face them with courage, wisdom, and an open heart.

The magical note pulsed gently under his pillow, as if acknowledging his readiness and preparing him for the final chapters of his extraordinary adventure. As Jake fell into a deep sleep, he dreamed of endless possibilities and the power of making the right choices.

Chapter 9

The Note's Secret

A Moment of Truth

As Jake sat on his bed, turning the magical note over in his hands, he couldn't help but feel a sense of anticipation. After all the adventures and challenges he'd faced, he knew he was on the cusp of uncovering the note's true purpose. The worn edges and faded markings seemed to pulse with an energy that was both exciting and slightly intimidating.

"I've come so far," Jake whispered to himself, "but there's still so much I don't understand."

The Unexpected Visitor

Just as Jake was about to place the note back in its hiding spot, a soft knock on his bedroom window startled him. To his amazement, the mysterious stranger he had encountered earlier was perched on the windowsill, gesturing for Jake to let him in.

With a mix of curiosity and caution, Jake opened the window. "Who are you?" he asked, his voice barely above a whisper.

The stranger smiled warmly. "I'm the Keeper of the Note, Jake. And it's time you learned its true purpose."

The Keeper's Tale

As Jake settled into his desk chair, the Keeper began to weave a tale that seemed almost too fantastical to believe. "The note you hold," he explained, "is not just a piece of currency. It's a test, a tool, and a teacher all rolled into one."

The Keeper went on to describe how the note had been created centuries ago by a group of wise elders who were concerned about the growing selfishness and greed in the world. They imbued the note with magical properties, allowing it to appear to those who had the potential to make a difference in the world.

"But why me?" Jake asked, his voice tinged with both wonder and confusion.

The Keeper's eyes twinkled. "Because, Jake, you have a heart that's open to learning and growing. The note chose you because it saw your potential to understand its lessons and share them with others."

The Power of Choice

As Jake listened intently, the Keeper explained that the note's magic wasn't just about providing endless wealth. Its true power lay in the choices it presented and the lessons it taught. "Think back on your journey, Jake," the Keeper urged. "What have you learned?"

Jake closed his eyes, remembering each encounter, each decision he had made. "I've learned about empathy," he said slowly, "and the importance of helping others. I've discovered the value of self-control and setting priorities."

The Keeper nodded encouragingly. "Go on."

"I've learned about loyalty and problem-solving," Jake continued, his voice growing stronger. "And I've realised that there are better ways to handle conflicts than seeking revenge."

"Excellent," the Keeper said, his smile widening. "And what about your experiences at the community fair?"

Jake's face lit up. "That was when I truly understood the joy of giving selflessly and being part of a community."

The Ultimate Lesson

The Keeper leaned forward, his expression serious. "And what about your greatest temptation, Jake? What did you learn when you were offered the chance to become incredibly wealthy?"

Jake paused, considering his words carefully. "I learned that true happiness doesn't come from having everything you want," he said slowly. "It comes from being content with what you have and using what you've been given to help others."

The Keeper clapped his hands together. "Precisely! And that, Jake, is the ultimate secret of the note. Its purpose isn't to make you rich or to solve all your problems. Its purpose is to teach you how to live a life of meaning, compassion, and wisdom."

The Note's True Nature

As Jake digested this information, the Keeper gently took the note from his hands. To Jake's amazement, the markings on the note began to shift and change, revealing a series of intricate patterns and symbols.

"What you see now," the Keeper explained, "is the true nature of the note. Each symbol represents a lesson you've learned, a challenge you've overcome. The note has been recording your journey all along."

Jake stared in awe at the transformed note. He could see images that reminded him of the homeless man, his friend in need, the bully, and all the other experiences he'd had. "It's like a map of my adventure," he breathed.

The Keeper nodded. "Indeed, it is. And now that you've uncovered its secret, you have a choice to make."

The Crossroads

Jake looked up, curiosity etched on his face. "What kind of choice?"

The Keeper's expression grew solemn. "Now that you understand the note's purpose, you must decide what to do with this knowledge. Will you keep the note, continuing to learn and grow? Or will you pass it on to someone else who might benefit from its lessons?"

Jake felt a weight settle on his shoulders. This was a big decision, perhaps the biggest he'd ever faced. "What happens if I keep it?" he asked.

"If you choose to keep the note," the Keeper explained, "you'll continue to face challenges and opportunities for growth. The note will guide you, helping you become an even better version of yourself."

"And if I give it away?"

The Keeper smiled. "Then you'll be giving someone else the chance to embark on their own journey of self-discovery and growth. You'll be passing on the wisdom you've gained and trusting that the note will find its way to someone who needs its guidance."

Reflection and Realisation

Jake fell silent, his mind whirling with thoughts and emotions. He thought about all he had experienced, all he had learned. He remembered the joy he felt when helping others, the sense of accomplishment when he overcame temptation, and the deep satisfaction of making the right choices even when they were difficult.

As he reflected, Jake began to realise something profound. The note had changed him, yes, but the change had come from within. The magic hadn't made his decisions for him or forced him to be a better person. It had simply provided opportunities for him to grow, to learn, and to become more aware of the impact his choices had on himself and others.

"I think I understand now," Jake said slowly, looking up at the Keeper. "The real magic isn't in the note at all, is it? It's in the choices we make and the lessons we learn from them."

The Keeper's eyes shone with pride. "You've grasped the deepest secret of all, Jake. The note is a tool, a guide, but the true power has been within you all along."

The Ripple Effect

As this realisation sank in, Jake began to see his adventures in a new light. Each decision he had made, each person he had helped, had created a ripple effect of positivity in the world around him.

He thought about the homeless man, wondering how that simple act of kindness might have changed his day or even his life. He remembered his friend and how solving that problem together had strengthened their bond. The bully, too, came to mind, and Jake wondered if their encounter had made any impact on the boy's behaviour.

"It's amazing," Jake mused aloud, "how one small action can lead to so much change."

The Keeper nodded sagely. "That's the beauty of it, Jake. Every choice we make, no matter how small it seems, has the potential to create positive change in the world. The note simply makes those choices more visible, more immediate."

The Power of Everyday Magic

As Jake continued to ponder, he began to see instances of "everyday magic" all around him. He thought of his parents, working hard to provide for the family. He remembered his teacher, staying late to help students who were struggling. Even the crossing guard at his school, who always had a friendly word for everyone, seemed magical in her own way.

"I'm starting to see that this kind of magic is everywhere," Jake said, his eyes wide with wonder. "People helping each other, making tough choices, trying to do the right thing... it's all around us, isn't it?"

The Keeper beamed. "Exactly! The note's magic is spectacular, but it's not unique. Every day, people all over the world are making choices that change lives and shape the future. They may not have a glowing piece of currency to guide them, but they're creating magic all the same."

The Weight of Knowledge

As this new understanding settled over him, Jake felt a mix of excitement and responsibility. He now saw the world through new eyes, recognising the potential for positive change in every interaction, every decision.

But with this knowledge came a weighty question: What should he do next?

"I feel like I should do something big," Jake admitted. "Now that I know all this, shouldn't I try to change the world in some huge way?"

The Keeper shook his head gently. "The desire to make a big impact is admirable, Jake, but remember true change often starts small. The most powerful transformations often begin with simple, everyday actions."

The Path Forward

As Jake pondered this advice, he began to see a path forward. He didn't need to change the world overnight. Instead, he could focus on making positive choices in his daily life, on being more aware of how his actions affected others, and on encouraging those around him to do the same.

"I think I know what I want to do," Jake said, his voice filled with quiet determination. "I want to keep learning and growing, but I also want to share what I've learned with others."

The Keeper nodded approvingly. "And how do you plan to do that?"

Jake's mind raced with possibilities. "I could start a club at school focused on community service. Or maybe I could write about my experiences to inspire others to make positive choices. And in my everyday life, I can be more mindful of how I treat people and how I can help make their days a little better."

The Decision

As Jake outlined his ideas, he felt a sense of clarity washing over him. He looked down at the magical note, still shimmering with its hidden symbols, and made his decision.

"I think," he said slowly, "that it's time for the note to find someone else who needs its guidance."

The Keeper's eyes twinkled. "Are you sure, Jake? Remember, there's no right or wrong choice here."

Jake nodded, feeling more certain by the moment. "I'm sure. The note has taught me so much, and I'll always be grateful for that. But now I think I'm ready to apply those lessons on my own, without their magic. And maybe someone else out there needs its help, just like I did."

Passing the Torch

With a mix of sadness and excitement, Jake handed the note back to the Keeper. As their hands touched, Jake felt a warm glow spread through him, as if the note was saying goodbye.

"You've made a noble choice, Jake", the Keeper said, his voice filled with pride. "By letting go of the note, you're demonstrating that you've truly understood its most important lesson: that the power to create positive change lies within you, not in any external object or force."

Jake smiled, feeling a sense of accomplishment wash over him. "Will I ever see the note again?" he couldn't help asking.

The Keeper chuckled. "Who knows? The ways of magic are mysterious. But whether you see this particular note again or not, I have a feeling you'll be creating plenty of magic of your own."

A New Chapter Begins

As the Keeper prepared to leave, Jake felt a mixture of emotions swirling within him. There was a touch of sadness at saying goodbye to the magical note that had been his companion through so many adventures. But overshadowing that was a sense of excitement and purpose.

"Before I go," the Keeper said, "Remember this, Jake: the end of one journey is often the beginning of another. The note's physical presence in your life may be ending, but the real adventure – living out the lessons you've learned – are just beginning."

Jake nodded, feeling a swell of determination. "I'm ready," he said simply.

With a final smile and a nod, the Keeper slipped out of the window and vanished into the night, taking the magical note with him.

Embracing the Future

Left alone in his room, Jake took a deep breath, feeling like he was on the brink of something new and exciting. The magical note was gone, but its lessons remained, etched into his heart and mind.

He walked to his desk and pulled out a fresh notebook. On the first page, he began to write: "The Adventures of The Boy and The Magic Money"

As he wrote, Jake smiled to himself. He may not have the note anymore, but he had something even more valuable: the knowledge, experience, and determination to make a positive difference in the world, one small choice at a time.

As he penned the first words of his story, Jake knew that this was just the beginning of a new and exciting chapter in his life—one filled with everyday magic, meaningful choices, and the power to inspire change in himself and others.

The magical note had served its purpose. Now, it was up to Jake to carry its lessons forward and create his kind of magic in the world.

Chapter 10

The Right Choice

The Weight of Responsibility

As Jake sat on the edge of his bed, the magical note resting in his palm, he felt the weight of responsibility pressing down on his shoulders. The journey that had begun with a torn piece of currency had led him through a series of challenges, each one teaching him valuable lessons about life, money, and what truly matters. Now, he faced his final and most crucial decision: what to do with the magical note that had changed his life forever.

You might think that having a magical note that could seemingly solve any problem would be a dream come true, but as Jake had learned, with great power comes great responsibility. He remembered all the moments that had brought him to this point, each memory vivid and charged with emotion.

Reflections on the Journey

Jake's mind wandered to his first encounter with the homeless man. He remembered his initial hesitation, the internal struggle between self-interest and compassion. "I could have easily walked away," he murmured to himself. "But choosing to help him taught me that true wealth isn't just about having." money—it's about using what you have to make a difference."

The toy store incident flashed before his eyes next. Jake chuckled softly, recalling how tempted he had been to buy everything his heart desired. "I thought having all those toys would make me happy," he mused. "But in the end, I realised that stuff doesn't bring lasting joy. It's the experiences and the people we share them with that count."

His thoughts then turned to his best friend and their predicament together. Jake had learned the value of loyalty and creative problem-solving, finding a way to help without revealing the note's secret. "That was when I truly understood that money isn't always the answer," he reflected. "Sometimes, it's about being there for someone and using your mind to find solutions."

The confrontation with the school bully still made Jake's heart race slightly. He had been so close to using the note for revenge, but something had held him back. "Choosing the high road was tough," he admitted to himself. "But it taught me that responding to negativity with more negativity never solves anything. There's always a better way if you're willing to look for it."

Jake smiled as he remembered the community fair. The joy he had felt helping various people in need was unlike anything he had experienced. "That day showed me the real power of giving," he thought. "It's not about the amount you give, but the impact it has on others and how it makes you feel inside."

The ultimate temptation—the offer of incredible wealth—had been his greatest test. Jake had stood at the crossroads, faced with a decision that could have changed his life forever. "I came so close to giving in," he whispered. "But all the lessons I had learned along the way helped me see that true happiness doesn't come from having everything you want. It comes from being content with what you have and using it to help others."

The Moment of Truth

As these memories washed over him, Jake realised that each experience had prepared him for this moment. The note's true purpose had been revealed to him, and now he had to decide what to do with this knowledge and power.

Jake stood up and walked to his window, gazing out at the neighbourhood he had grown up in. He saw the park where he and his friends played, the school where he learned, and the community centre that brought everyone together. In that moment, he understood that the magic of the note wasn't in its ability to create money out of thin air—it was in its power to teach, guide, and inspire.

"What would you do?" Jake asked, turning to face you, the reader. "If you had a magical note that could solve any problem, but you knew that keeping it might tempt you to use it for the wrong reasons, what choice would you make?"

The Decision

Jake took a deep breath and closed his eyes. When he opened them, there was a new determination in his gaze. He knew what he had to do.

With careful hands, Jake folded the magical note into a paper airplane. He opened his window and let the cool breeze caress his face. With a gentle push, he launched the paper airplane into the air.

As it soared away, carried by the wind, Jake felt a mix of emotions. There was a tinge of sadness at letting go of something so powerful, but it was overwhelmed by relief and rightness. He knew in his heart that this was the correct choice.

"The note has taught me everything it can," Jake said aloud, his voice steady and sure. "Now it's time for someone else to learn from it. Maybe it'll find its way to someone who needs its lessons just as much as I did."

Legacy of Learning

As the paper airplane disappeared from sight, Jake turned back to his room. He walked to his desk and pulled out a fresh notebook. On the first page, he began to write:

"The Adventures of the Magical Money: Lessons Learned"

Jake realised that although he no longer possessed the magical note, he still had something incredibly valuable—the wisdom and experiences he had gained. By writing down his story and his lessons, he could share that knowledge with others.

"I may not have the power to create money anymore," Jake thought, "but I can still make a difference by sharing what I've learned. Maybe my story can help others make better choices about money and life."

A New Chapter Begins

As Jake continued to write, he felt a sense of excitement growing within him. He wasn't just letting go of the magical note but embarking on a new adventure. An adventure of sharing, teaching, and continuing to learn.

He thought about all the people in his community—his friends, family, even strangers he had yet to meet. Each of them could benefit from the lessons he had learned. Jake realised that he wasn't ending his journey by letting go of the magical note—he was beginning a new one.

"I could have kept the note," Jake mused, his pen flying across the page. "I could have used it to become rich or famous. But what good is all the money in the world if you don't know how to use it wisely? What I've gained is worth more than any amount of magical money."

The Ripple Effect

As days turned into weeks and weeks into months, Jake saw the impact of his decision ripple out into the world around him. He shared his story with friends, who shared it with others. He volunteered at the community centre, teaching classes on financial responsibility and the importance of giving back.

Jake noticed changes in his community. People seemed more willing to help each other, more conscious of their spending habits, and more appreciative of what they had. It wasn't always easy, and there were still challenges, but there was a new sense of unity and purpose.

"It's amazing," Jake thought one day as he watched a group of kids organising a fundraiser for the local animal shelter. "All of this started with one magical note, but it's grown into something so much bigger. It's like the magic has spread to everyone but differently."

Lessons for Life

As you read Jake's story, you might be wondering what lessons you can take away from his journey. Here are a few key points to consider:

1. Money is a tool, not a goal: Jake learned that having money isn't as important as knowing how to use it wisely and for the benefit of others.

2. Generosity brings its own rewards: The joy Jake felt when helping others was more fulfilling than any material possession.

3. Temptation is a test of character: Throughout his journey, Jake faced numerous temptations. Each time he chose the right path, he grew stronger and wiser.

4. Problems often have solutions beyond money: Jake discovered that creativity, kindness, and perseverance can solve many problems that money can't.

5. True wealth is measured in experiences and relationships: The memories Jake made and the connections he formed were far more valuable than any amount of magical money.

6. Knowledge shared is knowledge multiplied: By choosing to share what he learned, Jake created a lasting impact that went far beyond what he could have achieved alone.

7. The right choice isn't always the easy choice: Letting go of the magical note was difficult, but Jake knew it was the right thing to do.

The Ongoing Journey

As Jake's story spread, it inspired others to examine their own relationships with money and values. People began to ask themselves important questions:

- What truly brings happiness and fulfilment in life?

- How can I use my resources to make a positive impact on the world?

- What lessons am I teaching others through my actions and choices?

These questions didn't always have easy answers, but the very act of asking them and reflecting on them led to positive changes in individuals and communities.

A Message to You, the Reader

Now, as you reach the end of Jake's story, it's time to turn the spotlight on yourself. What magical notes exist in your own life? These might not be literal pieces of currency with supernatural powers, but they could be talents, opportunities, or resources that you possess.

Ask yourself:

- How can I use what I have to make a positive difference in the world?
  - What lessons have I learned about money and values that I can share with others?
  - In what ways can I contribute to my community and help create a ripple effect of positive change?

Remember, every choice you make, no matter how small it may seem, has the potential to create a significant impact. Like Jake, you have the power to shape not only your own story but also to influence the stories of those around you.

The Never-Ending Story

As the sun set on another day, Jake closed his notebook and looked out his window. The world outside seemed different now—not because it had changed, but because he had. He saw opportunities where before he had seen obstacles, potential where he had once seen limitations.

"The adventure of the magical money might be over," Jake said softly, "but the real adventure—the adventure of life—is just beginning."

And with that thought, Jake stood up, ready to face whatever challenges and opportunities tomorrow might bring. He knew that while he no longer had a magical note in his pocket, he carried something far more valuable within his heart—the lessons, experiences, and wisdom gained from his extraordinary journey.

As you close this book and return to your own life, remember Jake's story. Let it inspire you to look at the world with new eyes, to make choices that align with your values, and to use whatever "magical notes" you possess to create positive change in your life and the lives of others.

After all, the true magic was never in the note itself. It was, and always will be, in the choices we make and the lives we touch along the way.

Chapter 11

The Courtroom Crucible

First Experiences in Mock Trials

As I stepped into the mock courtroom for the first time, my heart raced with a mixture of excitement and trepidation. The polished wooden benches, the imposing judge's seat, and the jury box all seemed to loom larger than life. This was it—the moment I had been working towards since I first dreamed of becoming a lawyer. But as I felt the familiar tightness in my throat, I wondered if I had made a terrible mistake.

You see, for someone with a stammer, the courtroom is the ultimate arena of verbal combat. Every word, every inflection, every pause can make or break your case. And here I was, about to put myself to the test in front of my peers and professors.

The first mock trial was a disaster. As I stood to deliver my opening statement, my stammer took hold with a vengeance. Words that I had practised countless times in front of my mirror became trapped behind an invisible barrier. I could see the pity in the eyes of my classmates, the impatience in the expression of the mock judge. By the time I finished, I was drenched in sweat and convinced that I had just witnessed the death of my legal career before it had even begun.

But something unexpected happened that day. As I slumped back into my seat, feeling utterly defeated, my trial partner leaned over and whispered, "That took guts. You didn't give up. We'll work on it together." Those simple words of encouragement were like a lifeline thrown to a drowning man. They reminded me why I had come this far, why I had refused to let my stammer define me all these years.

From that day forward, I approached each mock trial not as a test to be dreaded, but as an opportunity to grow. I began to see these simulated courtroom experiences as a safe space to experiment, to fail, and most importantly, to learn.

Strategies to Manage Stammer in High-Pressure Situations

Overcoming my stammer in the high-pressure environment of a courtroom—even a simulated one—required more than just willpower. It demanded a strategic approach, one that I developed through trial and error, consultation with speech therapists, and countless hours of practice.

One of the first techniques I employed was visualisation. Before each mock trial, I would spend time imagining myself in the courtroom, speaking clearly and confidently. I visualised not just the words coming out smoothly, but also the reactions of the judge, jury, and opposing counsel. This mental rehearsal helped to reduce my anxiety and build my confidence.

Another strategy that proved invaluable was controlled breathing. I learned to take deep, deliberate breaths before speaking, which helped to relax my vocal cords and reduce the likelihood of stammering. During particularly challenging moments, I would pause briefly, taking a moment to reset my breathing and gather my thoughts. What initially felt like awkward silences soon became powerful tools for emphasis and dramatic effect.

I also developed a system of subtle physical cues to help me maintain fluency. A light tap of my finger against my leg became a secret signal to myself to slow down and enunciate clearly. A slight shift in my stance helped to ground me when I felt my stammer threatening to take over.

Perhaps the most crucial strategy I developed was the art of preparation. I learned to anticipate potential stumbling blocks in my speech and develop workarounds. If there was a particular word or phrase that consistently gave me trouble, I would find alternative ways to express the same idea. This not only helped me to speak more fluently but also expanded my vocabulary and improved my overall communication skills.

But the real breakthrough came when I stopped trying to eliminate my stammer entirely and instead focused on working with it. I began to view my speech pattern not as a flaw to be hidden, but as a unique aspect of my communication style. This shift in perspective was liberating. It allowed me to focus on the content of my arguments rather than obsessing over every syllable.

Building Confidence in Legal Argumentation

As I became more comfortable managing my stammer, in the mock courtroom, I was able to turn my attention to honing my legal argumentation skills. This was where the real challenge—and the real excitement—began.

I discovered that effective legal argumentation is about much more than just speaking clearly. It's about constructing a compelling narrative, anticipating counterarguments, and thinking on your feet. In many ways, my years of dealing with a stammer had unknowingly prepared me for this aspect of legal work.

You see, when you grow up with a speech impediment, you become acutely aware of the power of words. You learn to choose your words carefully, to make every syllable count. This precision of language served me well in crafting legal arguments. I found that I had a knack for distilling complex legal concepts into clear, concise statements that resonated with mock juries.

Moreover, my experience with stammering had taught me the importance of non-verbal communication. I learned to use eye contact, facial expressions, and body language to enhance my arguments and

connect with my audience. These skills proved invaluable in the courtroom, where a raised eyebrow or a well-timed gesture could be just as powerful as a perfectly delivered phrase.

As I gained confidence in my ability to manage my stammer and construct compelling arguments, I began to enjoy the challenge of mock trials. Each new case became an opportunity to test my skills, to push my boundaries, and to grow as an advocate.

One particular mock trial stands out in my memory. It was a complex patent infringement case, with technical details that made my head spin. As I prepared for the trial, I found myself struggling not just with my stammer, but with understanding and explaining the intricate details of the case.

The night before the trial, I was ready to throw in the towel. But then I remembered something my mentor had told me: "The best lawyers aren't the ones who know everything. They're the ones who know how to learn anything." With that in mind, I stayed up late, breaking down the technical jargon into simple analogies and clear explanations.

When I stood up to deliver my opening statement the next day, I felt a familiar tightness in my throat. But this time, instead of panicking, I took a deep breath and launched into my carefully prepared analogy. I compared the patent dispute to a chef's secret recipe, explaining how the defendant had essentially stolen the "secret ingredient" that made the plaintiff's invention unique.

To my surprise and delight, I saw understanding dawn on the faces of the mock jury. My stammer was still there, but it no longer dominated my delivery. Instead, it became almost rhythmic, adding emphasis to key points in my argument.

As the trial progressed, I found myself growing more confident with each objection I raised, each witness I cross-examined. By the time I delivered my closing argument, I was no longer thinking about my stammer at all. I was focused entirely on making my case, on persuading the jury with the strength of my arguments and the clarity of my reasoning.

When the mock jury returned a verdict in my client's favour, I felt a surge of pride unlike anything I had experienced before. It wasn't just about winning the case. It was about proving to myself that I could do this, that I could be an effective advocate despite—or perhaps even because of—my stammer.

Turning Perceived Weakness into Strength

As I progressed through my law school journey, I began to realise something profound: my stammer, which I had always viewed as my greatest weakness, was becoming one of my greatest strengths in the courtroom.

You might be wondering how a speech impediment could possibly be an asset for a lawyer. Let me explain.

First, my stammer taught me the value of preparation. Because I knew that speaking off-the-cuff could be challenging, I always came to court meticulously prepared. I knew my cases inside and out, anticipated potential questions and objections, and had clear, concise responses ready. This level of preparation gave me a significant advantage, allowing me to present my arguments with confidence and respond effectively to unexpected challenges.

Secondly, my stammer made me a better listener. When you struggle to speak, you learn to appreciate the power of listening. In the courtroom, this translated into an ability to really hear what witnesses, opposing counsel, and judges were saying. I picked up on nuances and subtleties that others might miss, which often provided crucial insights for my cases.

Thirdly, my speech pattern, which I had once tried so hard to hide, became a tool for emphasising key points. A slight stammer on a crucial word could actually draw attention to it, making it more memorable for the jury. What I once saw as disruptive pauses became dramatic pauses, building tension and anticipation in my arguments.

Perhaps most importantly, my journey with stammering had given me a unique perspective on resilience and perseverance. Every time I stood up to speak in court, I was demonstrating to the jury that I had overcome significant challenges to be there. This unspoken testimony to my determination and commitment often worked in my favour, earning me respect and credibility with judges and juries alike.

I remember one particularly gruelling cross-examination where opposing counsel tried to fluster me by interrupting and speaking over me. In the past, this would have exacerbated my stammer and thrown me off balance. But now, I calmly waited for him to finish, then said, "Your Honour, as you can hear, I sometimes need a moment to get my words out. I'd appreciate if counsel could extend me that courtesy." The judge agreed, admonishing the other lawyer, and from that moment on, I controlled the pace of the questioning.

This incident taught me an important lesson: by openly acknowledging my stammer, I could take control of the narrative. Instead of allowing others to see it as a weakness, I presented it as simply another facet of who I was as an advocate.

Embracing Authenticity in the Courtroom

As I became more comfortable with my stammer in the courtroom, I made a conscious decision to embrace authenticity in my legal practice. I realised that trying to hide or completely overcome my stammer was not only exhausting but also counterproductive. Instead, I chose to be open about it and incorporate it into my professional identity.

This decision was not an easy one. The legal profession, especially in the courtroom, often seems to demand a certain type of polished, rapid-fire delivery that I couldn't always provide. But I reasoned that clients, juries, and judges would respond better to an authentic, albeit sometimes stammering, version of myself than to a facade of fluency that could crumble under pressure.

To my surprise, this approach resonated strongly with many people. Clients appreciated my honesty and often felt more comfortable opening up to me about their own vulnerabilities. Juries seemed to connect with me on a more human level, seeing beyond the legal arguments to the person making them.

I recall one case where I was representing a small business owner in a dispute with a large corporation. During my opening statement, I had a particularly noticeable stammer when introducing my client.

Instead of trying to gloss over it, I paused, smiled, and said, "As you can hear, ladies and gentlemen, sometimes my passion for my clients' cases makes my words a little eager to come out. But I assure you, by the end of this trial, you'll understand why I'm so passionate about seeing justice done for my client."

This moment of vulnerability and humour seemed to endear me to the jury. Throughout the trial, I noticed them paying close attention to my arguments, nodding along even when I took a moment to work through a difficult word. In the end, we won the case, and afterwards, one of the jurors approached me to say that my obvious determination to advocate for my client despite my stammer had been very powerful.

Experiences like these reinforced my belief that authenticity could be a powerful tool in the courtroom. By being open about my stammer, I was able to build trust and connection in a way that might not have been possible if I had tried to present a 'perfect' facade.

The Power of Persistence

As I neared the end of law school and looked back on my journey through mock trials and simulated courtroom experiences, I was struck by how far I had come. From that first disastrous attempt at an opening statement to confidently arguing complex cases, I had undergone a transformation that went far beyond just managing my stammer.

The key to this transformation, I realised, was persistence. Every time I stumbled over a word, every time I felt the frustration of not being able to express myself as quickly as I wanted, I had a choice. I could give up, or I could keep going. And time and time again, I chose to keep going.

This persistence paid off in ways I couldn't have imagined when I first started law school. Not only had I developed strategies to manage my stammer in high-pressure situations, but I had also honed my legal skills to a level that could compete with any of my fluent-speaking classmates.

More than that, I had discovered a depth of resilience within myself that I never knew existed. Each mock trial, each oral argument, each presentation was a testament to my determination to succeed despite the obstacles in my path.

As I prepared for my final mock trial of law school, I reflected on this journey. I thought about that scared, stammering student who had stood up for his first mock trial, certain that he was witnessing the end of his dreams. I wished I could go back and tell him that it wasn't the end, but the beginning. That each struggle, each moment of frustration, each small victory was shaping him into the advocate he was meant to be.

Standing up for that final mock trial, I felt a sense of calm confidence that would have been unimaginable to my younger self. As I began my opening statement, I could feel my stammer there, a familiar presence. But now, instead of fighting it, I worked with it, letting it add emphasis and humanity to my words.

I argued my case with passion and precision, weaving together the legal theories and practical skills I had learned over the years. When I finished my closing argument, there was a moment of silence in the mock courtroom. Then, to my surprise, my classmates and the professors serving as judges burst into applause.

In that moment, I realised that I had done more than just learn to manage my stammer in the courtroom. I had learned to thrive because of it. My journey had taught me resilience, empathy, and the power of authenticity – lessons that would serve me well not just in my legal career, but in life.

As I left the mock courtroom for the last time, I felt ready to face the challenges of a real courtroom. I knew that there would be difficult moments ahead, times when my stammer might make things harder than they would be for other lawyers. But I also knew that I had the tools, the skills, and most importantly, the determination to overcome these challenges.

My time in law school had transformed the courtroom from a place of fear into an arena of possibility. It was no longer a crucible to be dreaded, but a platform where I could make a difference, where I could use my voice – stammer and all – to fight for justice and make a positive impact in the world.

Preparing for the Real-World

As law school drew to a close, and the prospect of entering the real legal world loomed, I found myself both excited and apprehensive. The mock trials and simulated courtroom experiences had been invaluable, but I knew that the stakes would be much higher when I was representing real clients with real problems.

I began to prepare for this transition with the same diligence and determination that had carried me through law school. I sought out internships and clerkships that would give me exposure to real courtroom proceedings. I observed as many trials as I could, paying close attention to the different styles and techniques employed by experienced attorneys.

One particularly enlightening experience came during an internship with a local public defender's office. I was assigned to assist on a case involving a young man accused of theft. As I sat in on client meetings and helped prepare for the trial, I was struck by the weight of responsibility we carried. This wasn't a mock trial where a mistake would only cost me a grade. This was a real person's life and future at stake.

The lead attorney on the case, a seasoned public defender named Maria, became a mentor to me during this time. She had a slight lisp, which she had long ago stopped trying to hide or correct. Watching her in court was a revelation. She used her distinctive speech pattern to her advantage, using it to capture the jury's attention and emphasise key points.

One day, after we had won a motion to suppress some evidence, I asked Maria how she had become so confident in her speaking style. She smiled and said, "Honey, it took me years to realise that this lisp is part of what makes me a damn good lawyer. It makes me memorable. It makes people listen more carefully. And it reminds everyone in that courtroom that I'm human, just like my clients."

Her words struck a chord with me. They reinforced what I had begun to learn in my mock trial experiences – that my stammer could be an asset rather than a liability in the courtroom.

As my internship progressed, Maria gave me more opportunities to speak in court – first in simple procedural matters, then in arguing motions, and finally in questioning witnesses during a trial. Each time I stood up to speak, I could feel the eyes of the judge, the jury, the opposing counsel upon me. But instead of shrinking from their gaze, I drew strength from it.

I remembered all the techniques I had developed during mock trials – the breathing exercises, the subtle physical cues, the careful word choices. But more than that, I channelled the confidence and authenticity that I had cultivated over the years.

There were still moments when my stammer got the better of me, times when a crucial question came out haltingly or when I had to pause to gather my thoughts mid-argument. But I had learned not to let these moments derail me. Instead, I would take a breath, sometimes even acknowledging my stammer with a small smile, and then continue with my point.

To my surprise, I found that these moments of vulnerability often seemed to work in my favour. Jurors would lean in, listening more intently. Judges would show patience, allowing me the time I needed to make my arguments. Even opposing counsel seemed less inclined to interrupt or object when I was speaking.

As the internship came to an end, I felt a new sense of readiness for the challenges ahead. I had tested my skills in real courtroom situations and found that I could hold my own. More than that, I had seen firsthand how my unique speaking style could be an asset in connecting with clients, jurors, and judges.

Maria's parting words to me stuck with me long after the internship ended. "Remember," she said, "the most powerful tool you have in that courtroom isn't your voice – it's your conviction. Believe in yourself and in your client, and you'll find the words you need, stammer or no stammer."

Embracing the Journey Ahead

As I stood on the cusp of my legal career, diploma in hand and bar exam behind me, I took a moment to reflect on the journey that had brought me to this point. From that first disastrous mock trial to arguing real cases in court, I had come further than I ever thought possible when I first dreamed of becoming a lawyer.

The courtroom, once a source of fear and anxiety, had become a place where I felt empowered and alive. My stammer, once my greatest perceived weakness, had become a unique strength, helping me to connect with clients, jurors, and judges on a human level.

I knew that the road ahead would not be easy. There would be challenging cases, difficult clients, and opposing counsel who might try to use my stammer against me. But I also knew that I was prepared for. these challenges. I had the legal knowledge, the courtroom skills, and most importantly, the resilience and determination to overcome whatever obstacles lay ahead.

As I prepared for my first day as a practicing attorney, I made a promise to myself. I vowed to never forget the lessons I had learned during my time in law school and my internships. I promised to always strive for authenticity, to use my unique voice to advocate for those who needed it most, and to never let my stammer hold me back from pursuing justice.

The courtroom crucible had tested me, challenged me, and ultimately forged me into the advocate I had always dreamed of becoming. As I stepped into the next chapter of my journey, I did so not in spite of my stammer, but because of it. It had taught me perseverance, empathy, and the power of embracing one's authentic self.

I was ready to face whatever challenges lay ahead, armed with the knowledge that my voice – stammer and all – had the power to make a difference in the world. The courtroom awaited, and I was eager to step into the arena, ready to fight for justice, one carefully chosen word at a time.

Chapter 12

Beyond Words

The Power of Non-Verbal Communication

As I stood before the mirror, practicing my opening statement for an upcoming case, I realised something profound. My words, though carefully chosen and rehearsed, were only part of the story. There was an entire language beyond speech that I had yet to fully explore and harness.

You see, for someone like me who has struggled with a stammer for most of my life, the concept of communication has always been a complex one. I've spent years focusing on my words, trying to control and perfect them. But in that moment of reflection,

I understood that true communication goes far beyond the syllables we utter.

This chapter is about that journey – the discovery and development of non-verbal communication skills that would not only complement my speech but also become a powerful tool in their own right. It's about learning to use body language and presence to command attention, and ultimately, turning what I once perceived as a weakness into one of my greatest strengths.

The Silent Language of the Body

Have you ever noticed how some people can captivate a room without saying a word? It's as if they have an invisible aura that draws others in. This, my friends, is the power of body language.

When I first began to explore this concept, I was sceptical. How could I, someone who struggled to get words out, possibly command attention through my body? But as I delved deeper, I realised that this was precisely why non-verbal communication could be so powerful for me.

I started small, focusing on my posture. Standing tall, shoulders back, chin up – it felt unnatural at first,

almost like I was trying to be someone else. But the results were immediate and surprising. People seemed to pay more attention to me, even before I started speaking.

Next, I worked on my facial expressions. As someone who had spent years trying to hide my stammer, I had developed a habit of keeping my face neutral, almost blank. I practised expressing emotions more openly – letting my face show interest, concern, or conviction depending on the situation.

One particularly memorable moment came during a pre-trial conference. As opposing counsel was speaking, I maintained steady eye contact and nodded thoughtfully at key points. When it was my turn to respond, I paused, took a deep breath, and leaned in slightly before speaking. The judge, who had seemed distracted earlier, now gave me his full attention. It wasn't just about the words I was about to say; it was about the presence I had created.

The Art of the Pause

In my journey to overcome my stammer, I had always seen pauses as the enemy. They were moments of vulnerability, gaps where my speech might falter. But as I delved deeper into non-verbal communication, I began to see pauses in a new light.

A well-timed pause, I learned, could be incredibly powerful. It could create anticipation, emphasise a point, or give the listener time to absorb what had been said. For me, it also provided a moment to gather my thoughts and control my speech.

I remember the first time I deliberately used a pause in court. I was arguing a motion, and I had just made a key point. Instead of rushing to my next argument, as I would have done in the past, I paused. I maintained eye contact with the judge, letting the silence fill the room for a few seconds. The effect was palpable. The judge leaned forward slightly, clearly waiting for what I would say next.

From that moment on, pauses became one of my most effective tools. I used them to punctuate important points, to transition between arguments, and sometimes, simply to command attention. What had once been a source of anxiety now became a source of power.

The Eyes Have It

They say the eyes are the windows to the soul, and in my experience, they're also one of the most powerful tools in non-verbal communication. Eye contact, when used effectively, can convey confidence, sincerity, and authority.

For someone with a stammer, maintaining eye contact can be challenging. There's often an instinct to look away, especially when struggling with a word. But I forced myself to overcome this tendency, practicing maintaining steady eye contact even when my speech faltered.

I started by practicing with friends and family, then moved on to professional settings. I remember one particular client meeting where this practice paid off. I was explaining a complex legal strategy, and I could feel my stammer threatening to emerge. Instead of looking down or away, I maintained eye contact with my client, even as I worked through a difficult word, I kept my gaze steady. After the meeting, the client commented on how confident and knowledgeable I seemed. It wasn't just about what I had said, but how I had said it – with my eyes as much as my words.

Gestures: The Silent Amplifiers

Have you ever watched a great public speaker and noticed how they use their hands? Gestures can emphasise points, illustrate concepts, and add energy to a presentation. For me, they became another way to communicate when words failed.

I began incorporating deliberate gestures into my courtroom presentations. A sweeping motion to indicate the scope of an issue, a firm hand gesture to drive home a point, open palms to convey honesty and openness – these became part of my legal vocabulary.

One particularly effective technique I developed was using gestures to bridge moments when I was struggling with a word. Instead of freezing up, I would use a deliberate hand motion, almost as if I was physically pulling the word out. This not only helped me get through difficult moments but also kept the audience engaged.

There was a pivotal moment in a high-stakes negotiation where this technique proved invaluable. I was presenting our final offer, and I could feel a challenging word coming up. Instead of tensing up, I used a firm, decisive hand gesture as I worked through the word. The opposing counsel later mentioned that this moment stood out to him – he said it conveyed a sense of unwavering conviction in our position.

The Power of Presence

As I continued to develop my non-verbal skills, I began to understand the concept of 'presence'. It's that indefinable quality that some people have – the ability to command attention and respect simply by being in a room.

For me, developing presence was about bringing together all the non-verbal skills I had been working on – posture, facial expressions, eye contact, gestures – and combining them with a sense of confidence and purpose.

I practised this presence everywhere – in client meetings, in the courtroom, even in social situations. It wasn't about being loud or dominant, but about being fully present and engaged in every interaction.

One of the most rewarding moments came during a pro bono case I was handling. My client, a young man facing unfair eviction, was clearly intimidated by the legal process. As we entered the courtroom, I made a conscious effort to project calm confidence through my body language. I stood tall, made respectful eye contact with the judge, and used measured gestures as I presented our case. I could see my client visibly relax and straighten up beside me. After the hearing, which went in our favour, he told me that seeing my confidence had helped him feel more secure.

Turning Weakness into Strength

Perhaps the most profound realisation in this journey was how my stammer, which I had always seen as a weakness, had actually driven me to develop these non-verbal skills. In focusing so intently on body language, presence, and non-verbal cues, I had developed a level of communication that went beyond words.

I began to see my stammer not as a handicap, but as the catalyst that had pushed me to become a more complete communicator. In some ways, it had given me an edge. While others relied primarily on their words, I had learned to use every tool at my disposal to connect with and persuade others.

This shift in perspective was liberating. Instead of trying to hide or overcome my stammer, I began to view it as part of my unique communication style. It was no longer about being 'normal' or 'fluent', but about being effective and authentic.

The Classroom Becomes the Courtroom

As I became more confident in my non-verbal skills, I decided to share what I had learned. I began offering workshops for other lawyers, particularly those who struggled with public speaking or courtroom anxiety.

In these workshops, I would often demonstrate the power of non-verbal communication through a simple exercise. I would deliver the same legal argument twice – once using only verbal communication, and once incorporating all the non-verbal techniques I had learned. The difference in impact was always striking.

Participants would comment on how much more convincing and authoritative I seemed in the second delivery, even though the words were exactly the same. It was a powerful illustration of how communication goes far beyond the words we speak.

The Silent Advocate

As my career progressed, I found that my non-verbal skills were often as crucial to my success as my legal knowledge. There were times when a well-timed pause or a confident stance swayed a judge more than any verbal argument could have.

I remember one particularly tense moment during a high-profile case. The opposing counsel had just made a strong argument, and the courtroom was buzzing. As I stood to respond, I took a moment to make eye contact with each member of the jury. I then turned to the judge, paused for a beat, and began my rebuttal with a calm, measured gesture. The room fell silent, and I could feel every eye on me. In that moment, before I had even spoken a word, I knew I had their attention and respect.

Beyond the Courtroom

The skills I developed didn't just serve me in professional settings. They transformed my personal interactions as well. In social situations where I once would have been hesitant to engage, I now felt confident. Even when my speech faltered, I could rely on my non-verbal skills to maintain connection and communication.

This newfound confidence spilled over into all areas of my life. I became more active in community organisations, took on speaking engagements about overcoming obstacles, and even began mentoring young lawyers who struggled with similar challenges.

One particularly memorable moment came when I was asked to give a keynote speech at a legal conference. As I stood on the stage, looking out at a sea of faces, I felt a moment of panic. But then I took a deep breath, straightened my posture, and began. Even when my stammer emerged, I maintained eye contact, used deliberate gestures, and let my passion for the subject show on my face. The response was overwhelming – not just applause, but a standing ovation.

The Ongoing Journey

As I reflect on this journey beyond words, I'm struck by how much it has transformed not just my communication, but my entire outlook on life. What began as a coping mechanism for my stammer has become a powerful set of skills that enhance every interaction.

But it's important to note that this isn't a destination I've reached, but an ongoing journey. Every day brings new opportunities to refine these skills, to connect more deeply with others, to communicate more effectively.

To you, dear reader, whether you struggle with a stammer or any other communication challenge, I want to say this: your voice is more than your words. Your ability to connect, to persuade, to lead – it comes from something deeper than speech. It comes from your presence, your confidence, your authenticity.

So stand tall. Make eye contact. Use your hands to emphasise your points. Let your face show your emotions. Embrace the power of the pause. And remember, every challenge you face is an opportunity to develop strengths you never knew you had.

As we move forward into the next chapter, where we'll explore my first real case, remember that the skills we've discussed here were crucial in that pivotal moment. The confidence I had developed in my non-verbal communication would be put to the ultimate test in a real courtroom, with real stakes. But that's a story for our next chapter.

Chapter 13

The First Real Case

The Weight of Reality

As I stood outside the courthouse, my palms were sweating, and my heart was racing. This wasn't a mock trial or a practice session. This was real. The weight of my first actual court appearance pressed down on me like a physical force. I took a deep breath, trying to calm my nerves and quiet the stammer that threatened to overwhelm me.

You might think that after all the preparation, all the practice, and all the progress I'd made, I'd be ready for this moment. But the truth is, nothing can truly prepare you for the first time you step into a courtroom as a practicing lawyer. The stakes are higher, the pressure more intense, and the consequences more real than anything you've experienced before.

Preparing for Battle

In the weeks leading up to this day, I had thrown myself into preparation with a fervour that bordered on obsession. Every waking moment was dedicated to reviewing case files, rehearsing arguments, and practicing my delivery. I knew that my stammer could be my downfall if I wasn't meticulously prepared.

You see, when you have a speech impediment, you can't afford to wing it. Every word, every phrase needs to be carefully chosen and practised. I spent hours in front of the mirror, watching my mouth form the words, focusing on the techniques I'd learned over the years to manage my stammer.

But it wasn't just about the words. I also had to prepare myself mentally and emotionally for the challenge ahead. I meditated, visualised success, and reminded myself of how far I'd come. You might be surprised at how much of legal work is psychological. It's not just about knowing the law; it's about believing in yourself and your ability to advocate for your client.

The Night Before

The evening before the trial, I couldn't sleep. My mind was racing, playing out every possible scenario. What if I stumbled over a crucial piece of evidence? What if my stammer got the better of me during cross-examination? What if the judge lost patience with my halting speech?

I tossed and turned, the silence of the night amplifying my fears. In those dark hours, doubt crept in, whispering that maybe I wasn't cut out for this after all. Maybe I should have chosen a career that didn't require so much speaking, so much public performance.

But then I remembered why I had chosen this path. I thought about all the people who had believed in me, supported me, and helped me get to this point. I thought about my client, who was counting on me to be their voice in the courtroom. And I thought about that young boy with a stammer who dreamed of becoming a lawyer, despite all the odds stacked against him.

I got out of bed and went to my desk. There, I wrote myself a letter of encouragement, pouring out all my fears and hopes onto the page. Writing has always been my refuge, my way of organising my thoughts and finding clarity. As I wrote, I felt my resolve strengthening. By the time I finished, the first light of dawn was peeking through my window, and I felt ready to face the day.

The Morning of the Trial

As I dressed in my carefully pressed suit, I went through my pre-trial routine. I did some breathing exercises to calm my nerves and loosen up my vocal cords. I practised some of the more challenging phrases from my opening statement, focusing on the techniques I'd learned to manage my stammer.

Before leaving my apartment, I looked at myself in the mirror. "You can do this," I told my reflection. "You've worked hard for this moment. Your stammer doesn't define you. Your passion, your knowledge, and your determination do."

With those words of self-encouragement, I grabbed my briefcase and headed to the courthouse.

Entering the Arena

The courthouse was bustling with activity when I arrived. Lawyers in suits rushed past, their briefcases swinging. Clients waited nervously on benches, whispering to their attorneys. The air was thick with tension and anticipation.

I made my way to the designated courtroom, my footsteps echoing in the marble hallway. As I approached, I saw my client waiting outside. Their face lit up with relief when they saw me, and I felt a renewed sense of purpose. This wasn't just about me and my stammer. This was about justice for my client.

"Are you ready?" they asked, their voice tinged with nervousness.

I nodded, managing a smile. "As ready as I'll ever be," I replied, proud that my voice didn't waver.

The Moment of Truth

As we entered the courtroom, the gravity of the situation hit me full force. The judge's bench loomed before us, imposing and authoritative. The jury box to the side was empty for now, but soon it would be filled with the people who would decide our fate.

I set up at the defence table, arranging my notes and documents with meticulous care. Each motion was deliberate, a way to channel my nervous energy and maintain my composure. My client sat beside me, their presence both a comfort and a reminder of the responsibility I carried.

The bailiff called the court to order, and suddenly, it was time. The judge entered, and we all rose. As I stood there, my heart pounding in my chest, I took a deep breath and reminded myself of all the work I'd done to get here.

Opening Statements

"The defence may present its opening statement."

Those words from the judge sent a jolt through me. This was it. The moment I'd been preparing for, dreaming of, and dreading in equal measure. I stood up, smoothed my jacket, and walked to the centre of the courtroom.

I faced the jury, my eyes sweeping over their faces. They looked back at me expectantly, waiting to hear what I had to say. In that moment, I felt a strange calm settle over me. All the preparation, all the practice, all the years of struggle and triumph - it all led to this moment.

I opened my mouth, and the words began to flow. "Ladies and gentlemen of the jury," I began, my voice clear and steady. "Today, we are here to examine the facts of this case..."

As I spoke, I could feel my stammer lurking at the edges of my speech, threatening to break through. But I didn't let it. I used every technique I'd learned, every ounce of concentration I possessed, to keep my words flowing smoothly.

I laid out our case, pointing out the weaknesses in the prosecution's argument and highlighting the evidence that supported our position. As I spoke, I could see the jurors leaning in, their expressions attentive. They weren't focused on how I was speaking, but on what I was saying.

When I finished my opening statement and returned to my seat, I felt a surge of triumph. I had done it. I had delivered a clear, compelling argument without letting my stammer get the better of me.

The Trial Unfolds

As the trial progressed, I found myself settling into a rhythm. Each time I stood to question a witness or object to the prosecution's line of questioning, it became a little easier. My stammer was still there, lurking beneath the surface, but I was managing it.

There were moments of difficulty, of course. During a particularly intense cross-examination, I felt my stammer threatening to break through. But instead of panicking, I paused, took a breath, and rephrased my question. The judge and jury didn't seem to notice anything amiss, and the witness answered my question without hesitation.

Throughout the trial, I kept reminding myself to focus on the case, not on my speech. I threw myself into the details of the evidence, the nuances of the law, and the strategy of our defence. By immersing myself in the work, I found that my stammer became less and less of an issue.

The Closing Argument

Before I knew it, it was time for closing arguments. As I stood to address the jury for the final time, I felt a mix of exhaustion and exhilaration. We had put up a strong defence, and now it was time to drive our points home.

I began my closing argument, weaving together the threads of evidence we had presented throughout the trial. As I spoke, I could feel the power of my words, the strength of our case. My voice was clear, my arguments precise. The stammer that had once defined me was nowhere to be heard.

As I concluded, I looked each juror in the eye. "Ladies and gentlemen," I said, my voice strong and confident, "Based on the evidence presented, I ask you to find my client not guilty. Thank you."

I returned to my seat, my heart pounding. I had done all I could. Now, it was up to the jury.

The Verdict

The wait for the jury's decision was agonising. My client and I sat in tense silence, each lost in our own thoughts. I replayed the trial in my mind, analysing every moment, wondering if I could have done anything differently.

Finally, the jury returned. As the foreman stood to read the verdict, I held my breath. "We, the jury, find the defendant... not guilty."

Relief and joy washed over me. We had won. My client turned to me, tears in their eyes, and whispered a heartfelt thank you. In that moment, all the years of struggle, all the doubts and fears, seemed worth it.

Reflection and Growth

As I left the courthouse that day, I felt like a different person than the one who had entered that morning. I had faced my greatest fear - speaking in public, in a high-stakes situation - and I had triumphed.

This case taught me that my stammer didn't have to be a liability. In fact, it had made me a better lawyer. The years of dealing with my speech impediment had taught me patience, perseverance, and the importance of thorough preparation. These skills had served me well in the courtroom.

Moreover, I realised that my journey with my stammer had given me a unique perspective. I understood what it was like to feel voiceless, to struggle to be heard. This understanding allowed me to connect with my client on a deeper level and to advocate for them with genuine empathy and passion.

Looking Ahead

As I reflected on my first real case, I knew that this was just the beginning. There would be more cases, more challenges, more opportunities to prove myself. But now, I faced the future with confidence. I had proven to myself, and to the world, that I could be a successful lawyer despite my stammer.

This case had been a crucible, testing everything I had learned and everything I believed about myself. I had emerged stronger, more confident, and more determined than ever to succeed in my chosen career.

As I walked away from the courthouse, I couldn't help but smile. The stuttering orphan who once struggled to say his own name had just won his first case as a practicing attorney. It was a victory not just for me, but for everyone who had ever been told they couldn't achieve their dreams because of a perceived limitation.

I knew there would be more challenges ahead. My stammer wasn't gone; it would always be a part of me. But I had proven that it didn't have to define me or limit me. With hard work, determination, and the right techniques, I could manage my stammer and be an effective advocate for my clients.

As I hailed a taxi to head back to my office, I felt a sense of excitement for what the future held. This first case was just the beginning. I was ready to take on whatever challenges came next, one word at a time.

Rising Through the Ranks

Building a Reputation

As I stepped out of the courtroom, my heart still racing from the adrenaline of my latest case, I couldn't help but reflect on how far I'd come. It wasn't long ago that the mere thought of speaking in public would send me into a tailspin of anxiety. Now, here I was, building a reputation as a competent lawyer, one case at a time.

You see, success in the legal world isn't just about winning cases. It's about consistency, reliability, and the ability to deliver results time and time again. For someone like me, who had battled a severe stammer for most of my life, this journey was nothing short of miraculous.

I remember the day I received my first referral from a colleague. It was a small case, nothing earth-shattering, but it meant the world to me. Someone had enough faith in my abilities to recommend me to their client. As I sat across from this new client, I felt a familiar tightness in my throat, that old nemesis threatening to resurface. But I took a deep breath, centred myself, and began to speak.

"I understand you're facing some challenges with your landlord," I said, my words coming out slowly, but steadily. "Let's go through the details, and I'll explain how we can approach this."

As I spoke, I saw the tension in the client's shoulders ease. They weren't focused on how I was speaking, but what I was saying. It was a revelation that would serve me well as I continued to climb the ranks in my profession.

Handling Increasingly Complex Cases

As my reputation grew, so did the complexity of the cases that came my way. Each new challenge pushed me to my limits, forcing me to adapt and grow not just as a lawyer, but as a communicator.

One particularly daunting case involved a multinational corporation accused of environmental violations. The sheer volume of documents to review was overwhelming, and the technical jargon involved was enough to tie anyone's tongue in knots, let alone someone with a stammer.

I spent countless nights poring over reports, practicing key phrases, and rehearsing my arguments. I knew that in court, every word would count. The opposing counsel was known for their aggressive tactics, and I couldn't afford to let my speech impediment become a weakness they could exploit.

The day of the first hearing arrived, and as I stood to address the court, I felt a familiar flutter of nervousness in my stomach. But along with it came a sense of readiness. I had prepared for this moment, and I was determined to let my expertise shine through.

"Your Honour," I began, my voice clear and steady, "the evidence will show that my client has not only adhered to all environmental regulations but has gone above and beyond in their commitment to sustainable practices."

As I laid out our case, I could see the judge leaning in, engaged by my arguments. The opposing counsel tried to interrupt, to throw me off my stride, but I held firm. My stammer, once my greatest weakness, had taught me the value of choosing my words carefully and speaking with intention.

By the end of the trial, we had secured a favorable outcome for our client. It wasn't just a victory in the legal sense; it was a personal triumph that showed me just how far I'd come.

Balancing Career Growth with Ongoing Speech Management

As my career continued to flourish, I found myself facing a new challenge: balancing the demands of an increasingly high-profile career with the ongoing need to manage my speech. Success hadn't cured my stammer; it had simply given me better tools to work with.

I began each day with a series of speech exercises, warming up my vocal cords and practicing difficult sounds. These routines, once a source of frustration and embarrassment, had become as natural to me as brushing my teeth or tying my shoes.

But as the cases grew more complex and the stakes higher, I found myself needing to adapt my strategies. Long days in court or marathon negotiation sessions could leave my speech fatigued, causing my stammer to become more pronounced.

I learned to pace myself, to take strategic pauses not just for dramatic effect, but to give myself moments to regroup and refocus. I developed a signal system with my legal team, subtle gestures that could indicate when I needed them to step in or when I was ready to take the lead again.

One particularly gruelling case taught me the importance of self-care in maintaining my speech fluency.

It was a high-stakes corporate merger, with long days of negotiations followed by nights of preparation. By the third day, I could feel my control slipping, words sticking in my throat more frequently.

That evening, instead of pushing through more preparation, I made a decision. I went back to my hotel room, ran a hot bath, and spent an hour doing relaxation exercises and gentle speech practice. The next morning, I felt refreshed, my speech flowing more easily.

As we entered the final day of negotiations, I felt a new sense of confidence. "Gentlemen," I said, addressing the room full of executives and lawyers, "I believe we have the framework for an agreement that will benefit all parties." My voice was strong, my words clear. The relief and pride I saw in my clients' eyes told me that my decision to prioritise my speech management had paid off.

Mentoring and Giving Back

As my reputation in the legal community grew, I found myself in a position I never thought possible: being sought out as a mentor by young lawyers and law students. Many were drawn to me not just for my legal expertise, but because they too struggled with speech impediments or other challenges that made them doubt their place in the legal profession.

I remember clearly the first time a young intern approached me after a court session. She was trembling slightly, her eyes downcast as she spoke.

"Mr. Johnson," she said, her voice barely above a whisper, "I... I have a st-stammer too. I've always wanted to be a lawyer, but seeing you in court today... it gave me hope."

Her words hit me like a thunderbolt. I realised that my journey wasn't just about my own success anymore. I had the power to inspire others, to show them that a stammer didn't have to be a career- ending obstacle.

From that day on, I made it a point to make time for these aspiring lawyers. I shared my experiences, my techniques for managing my speech in high-pressure situations, and most importantly, my belief in their abilities.

One of my proudest moments came when I received an invitation to speak at a law school's career day. As I stood at the podium, looking out at a sea of eager faces, I felt a moment of panic. This wasn't a courtroom; these weren't arguments I had rehearsed a hundred times. This was personal.

I took a deep breath and began. "When I was sitting where you are now," I said, my words coming slowly but clearly, "I never imagined I'd be standing here today. My stammer made me doubt whether I could ever be a lawyer. But what I've learned is that our challenges don't define us - how we overcome them does."

As I spoke, I could see nods of recognition, tears in some eyes, and a growing sense of possibility spreading through the room. It was a powerful reminder of why I had pushed myself so hard all these years.

Navigating Professional Relationships

As my career progressed, I found that managing professional relationships became increasingly important - and increasingly complex. My stammer, while much improved, was still a part of who I was, and learning to navigate it in various professional contexts became a crucial skill.

Client meetings, for instance, required a delicate balance. I needed to project confidence and expertise while also being honest about my speech. I developed a practice of addressing it upfront, usually with a touch of humour.

"Before we dive in," I'd say, "I want you to know that I sometimes stammer. It doesn't affect my ability to represent you, but it might affect how quickly I say 'objection' in court." This approach usually puts clients at ease and allows us to focus on the case at hand.

Networking events, a crucial part of building a legal career, presented their own challenges. The rapid-fire conversations and need for quick introductions could be particularly daunting. I learned to prepare a few key phrases about my work and interests, practicing them until they flowed smoothly. I also became adept at steering conversations towards topics where I felt more comfortable and fluent.

One particularly memorable networking event taught me the value of authenticity. I was speaking with a group of colleagues when I hit a difficult block on my own name. Instead of trying to push through or excuse myself, I paused, took a breath, and said with a smile, "Even after all these years, my name sometimes gives me trouble. Let me try that again." The understanding and respect I saw in their eyes was a powerful reminder that vulnerability can often be a strength.

Adapting to Technological Changes

As my career advanced, so did the technological landscape of the legal profession. E-discovery, video conferencing, and digital court filings became the norm, each bringing new challenges and opportunities for someone managing a stammer.

Video depositions, in particular, required a new set of skills. The lack of in person cues and the potential for technical glitches added an extra layer of complexity to managing my speech. I found that proper preparation was key. I would do a test run of the video setup, practice speaking to the camera, and ensure I had water and any other aids I might need close at hand.

One case involved a series of international video depositions, spanning multiple time zones. As I prepared for the first session, I felt a familiar knot of anxiety in my stomach. What if the connection dropped just as I was pushing through a difficult phrase? What if the delay made my speech pattern seem even more disjointed?

As the deposition began, I focused on speaking slowly and clearly, keeping my questions concise. To my surprise, I found that the slight delay in the video actually worked in my favour, giving me an extra moment to formulate my thoughts before speaking.

"Could you please elaborate on the events of May 15th?" I asked, my words coming out smoothly despite the complex technical setup. As the witness began to respond, I felt a surge of confidence. I was adapting, evolving, just as I had been doing since the start of my journey.

Handling Media Attention

As my reputation grew and I took on more high-profile cases, I found myself facing a new challenge: media attention. Suddenly, it wasn't just judges and juries I needed to convince, but reporters and cameras too.

My first major press conference was for a case involving a prominent local businessman accused of fraud. As I stood before the forest of microphones, I could feel my heart racing. This was different from a courtroom. There would be no objections, no rules of procedure to hide behind. Just me, my words, and a crowd of journalists eager for a sound bite.

I took a deep breath, centred myself, and began. "Good afternoon," I said, my voice steady despite the fluttering in my stomach. "We are here today to address the allegations against my client..."

As I spoke, I focused on the techniques I'd honed over years of practice. I maintained eye contact, varied my pace, and used strategic pauses not just to manage my stammer, but to emphasise key points. To my surprise, I found that the skills I'd developed to overcome my speech impediment were serving me well in this new arena.

The questions from reporters were rapid-fire, some clearly designed to provoke a reaction. But I had faced tougher opponents in court. I took each question in stride, answering clearly and concisely, never letting my stammer dictate the pace or content of my responses.

As the press conference ended, I felt a mix of exhaustion and exhilaration. I had faced one of my greatest fears - speaking unprepared in front of cameras - and had come through it successfully. It was a powerful reminder that the skills I'd developed weren't just about managing a stammer; they were about effective communication in any context.

Embracing Leadership Roles

As my career continued to advance, I found myself being offered leadership roles within my firm and in various legal associations. These positions presented new challenges, requiring me to not just argue cases, but to guide strategy, mentor younger lawyers, and represent the firm or organisation in various capacities.

My first major leadership role was as head of our firm's pro bono committee. It was a position that required not just legal expertise, but the ability to inspire and coordinate a team of busy lawyers to dedicate their time to worthy causes.

In our first committee meeting, I felt the familiar tightness in my throat as I prepared to outline our goals for the year. But as I looked around the table at my colleagues, I realised something important. They weren't there to judge my speech; they were there because they believed in the work we were doing and in my ability to lead it.

"Our goal this year," I said, my words coming slowly but with conviction, "is not just to meet our pro bono hours, but to make a real difference in our community." As I outlined our plans, I could see the enthusiasm building in the room. My stammer, far from being a hindrance, lent weight to my words. Each phrase was chosen carefully, delivered with intention.

Over time, I found that my journey with my stammer had equipped me with unique leadership skills. I was a patient listener, able to give others the time and space to express their ideas fully. I was adept at finding alternative ways to communicate when words failed, using visual aids or written summaries to reinforce key points.

Most importantly, I led with empathy. I understood what it was like to face challenges, to have to work harder than others to achieve the same results. This understanding allowed me to connect with my team on a deeper level, to inspire them not through grand speeches, but through genuine understanding and support.

Continuing Professional Development

Even as I rose through the ranks, I never lost sight of the importance of continuous learning and improvement. The legal field is constantly evolving, and staying at the top of my game required ongoing education and skill development.

I made it a point to attend conferences and workshops not just on legal topics, but on communication and public speaking as well. Each new technique I learned, whether it was a breathing exercise or a method for structuring arguments, became another tool in my arsenal for managing my speech and enhancing my effectiveness as a lawyer.

One particularly impactful workshop focused on the use of storytelling in legal arguments. The instructor emphasised the power of narrative to engage listeners and make complex legal concepts more accessible. For someone who had always relied on careful preparation and precise language to manage my stammer, the idea of telling stories in court was both exciting and terrifying.

I decided to put these new skills to the test in my next case, a complex contract dispute that hinged on the interpretation of a single clause. Instead of diving straight into legal jargon, I opened my argument with a story.

"Imagine, if you will," I began, my voice clear and measured, "two business partners shaking hands over a deal. They believe they understand each other perfectly. But as we'll see, words on paper can sometimes tell a different story."

As I wove the facts of the case into this narrative framework, I found myself speaking more fluently than ever before. The story carried me forward, each sentence flowing naturally into the next. By the time I reached my legal arguments, the judge was fully engaged, following my reasoning with keen interest.

This experience taught me that professional development wasn't just about learning new laws or precedents. It was about constantly expanding my communication toolkit, finding new ways to connect with judges, juries, and clients.

Reflecting on the Journey

As I look back on my journey from a stammering law student to a respected attorney rising through the ranks, I'm struck by how each challenge, each moment of doubt, has contributed to who I am today.

My stammer, once my greatest source of shame and anxiety, has become an integral part of my professional identity. It has taught me the value of preparation, the power of perseverance, and the importance of finding alternative paths when the direct route seems blocked.

More than that, it has given me a unique perspective on communication and advocacy. I understand, in a way that perhaps only those who have struggled with speech can, the true weight and power of words.

Every argument I make, every question I ask in court, comes from a place of deep consideration and intention.

As I continue to take on more complex cases and greater responsibilities, I carry with me the lessons learned from every stumbled word, every moment of panic overcome, every small victory won through sheer determination. These experiences have made me not just a better lawyer, but a more empathetic leader and a more effective advocate for my clients.

To those of you reading this who may be facing your own challenges, whether in the legal field or elsewhere, I want you to know this: your obstacles do not define you. They are not roadblocks, but opportunities for growth. Embrace them, learn from them, and let them fuel your journey to success.

As I look to the future, I'm excited for the challenges that lie ahead. Each new case, each leadership role, each public speaking engagement is an opportunity to further refine my skills and to show the world that a stammer is no barrier to excellence in the legal profession.

The journey from struggling with every word to confidently addressing courts and cameras has been long and often difficult. But standing here now, I can say with certainty that it has been worth every moment. And the best part? This journey is far from over. There are still heights to climb, challenges to overcome, and opportunities to seize.

So here's to the next chapter, to rising even higher through the ranks, and to continuing to prove that with determination, support, and the right strategies, any obstacle can be overcome. The courtroom awaits, and I'm ready to face whatever comes next, one carefully chosen word at a time.

Chapter 15

Advocacy Beyond Self

Becoming a Voice for Others

As I stood at the podium, my heart racing and palms sweating, I took a deep breath and reminded myself of how far I'd come. The journey from a stammering orphan to a successful lawyer had been long and arduous, but here I was, about to address a room full of aspiring lawyers and students with speech impediments. This moment wasn't just about me anymore; it was about becoming a voice for those who struggled to find their own.

I began my speech, and although the familiar tightness in my throat threatened to resurface, I pushed through. "I stand before you today not as someone who has conquered stammering, but as someone who has learned to coexist with it," I said, my voice steady and clear. "And I'm here to tell you that your voice matters, regardless of how it sounds."

The faces in the audience reflected a mix of hope, scepticism, and curiosity. I saw myself in their eyes – the same fears, the same doubts, and the same burning desire to be heard. It was at that moment I realised that my journey had led me to this new calling: advocating for those who faced the same challenges I had overcome.

Mentoring Young Lawyers and Students

My advocacy work began small, with one-on-one mentoring sessions with law students who stammered.

I remembered all too well the paralysing fear of being called on in class or the dread of upcoming oral arguments. Now, I could offer the guidance and support I wish I had received during those trying times.

One of my first mentees was Sarah, a brilliant second-year law student whose stammer had her questioning her choice of career. "I don't know if I can do this," she confided during our first meeting, her words punctuated by blocks and repetitions. "Maybe I should just stick to writing briefs and avoid courtroom work altogether."

I smiled, recognising the familiar self-doubt. "Sarah," I said gently, "Do you know how many times I had that exact same thought? But let me ask you this: why did you choose law in the first place?"

Her eyes lit up as she spoke about her passion for justice and her desire to make a difference. It was clear that her stammer hadn't diminished her eloquence or her convictions.

Over the next few months, we worked together on techniques to manage her stammer, build confidence, and prepare for oral arguments. I shared my own strategies – the breathing exercises, the visualisation techniques, and the importance of self-acceptance.

The day Sarah successfully delivered her first moot court argument was a victory for both of us. As she beamed with pride, I felt a sense of fulfilment that rivalled any courtroom win. This, I realised, was the true power of advocacy – empowering others to find their voice and pursue their dreams.

Public Speaking Engagements

As word spread about my mentoring work, invitations to speak at various events started pouring in. Law schools, speech therapy clinics, and even corporate diversity programmes wanted to hear my story and insights. Each invitation presented both an opportunity and a challenge – a chance to reach more people, but also a test of my own ongoing journey with stammering.

One particular event stands out in my memory. It was a TEDx talk titled "The Power of Imperfect Speech." As I prepared for it, I grappled with whether to try to hide my stammer completely or to intentionally let it show. After much reflection, I decided on authenticity.

On the day of the talk, I took the stage and began my speech. "I am a lawyer, an advocate, and a person who stammers," I said, allowing my stammer to manifest on the word "stammers.". The audience's surprise was palpable, but so was their engagement.

I went on to share my story, interspersing fluent speech with moments of stammering. I talked about the nights spent practicing in front of mirrors, the cruel taunts of classmates, and the triumphs in the courtroom. But more importantly, I spoke about the strength that comes from embracing one's unique voice.

"Fluency is not the only measure of effective communication," I said. "Authenticity, passion, and perseverance often speak louder than perfectly pronounced words."

The standing ovation that followed was overwhelming. But even more impactful were the conversations.

that came after – people sharing their own stories of struggle and triumph, not just with speech impediments, but with all manner of personal challenges.

Challenges and Growth

Becoming an advocate brought its own set of challenges. There were times when the pressure of being a role model felt overwhelming. What if I had a particularly bad day of stammering during an important speech? What if my advice didn't work for someone? The impostor syndrome that I thought I had left behind in my early law career reared its ugly head again.

I remember one particularly difficult day when I stumbled badly during a presentation at a national conference for speech-language pathologists. As I left the stage, feeling defeated, a young therapist approached me.

"Thank you," she said earnestly. "Seeing you struggle and continue anyway was the most powerful part of your presentation. It showed us all that it's not about being perfect; it's about being persistent."

Her words were a powerful reminder that advocacy isn't about presenting a flawless image. It's about showing the real, sometimes messy process of growth and resilience.

This realisation led me to be more open about my ongoing challenges with stammering. In my speeches and mentoring sessions, I began to share not just my successes, but also my setbacks. I talked about the days when words still failed me, the moments of frustration, and the ongoing work of self-acceptance.

This vulnerability, far from undermining my message, seemed to strengthen it. People connected more deeply with the honesty of my experiences, and it opened up more authentic dialogues about the complexities of living with a speech impediment.

Expanding the Scope

As my advocacy work grew, so did the scope of my efforts. What started as mentoring law students expanded to include working with children and teenagers who stammered. I partnered with schools to develop programmes that fostered understanding and support for students with speech impediments.

One initiative I'm particularly proud of is the "Speak Your Mind" programme, which we piloted in several high schools. The programme combines speech therapy techniques with confidence-building exercises and education about famous people throughout history who have struggled with stammering.

Watching young people transform from shy, reluctant speakers to confident communicators has been one of the most rewarding experiences of my life. I think of Maria, a 15-year-old who could barely introduce herself at the start of the programme. By the end, she was delivering a speech about her experiences to the entire school assembly.

"You taught me that my stammer is just one part of who I am," she told me afterward. "It doesn't define me or limit what I can achieve."

Advocacy in the Legal Profession

While my advocacy work extended beyond the legal profession, I remained committed to creating change within it. The law, with its emphasis on oral arguments and rapid-fire questioning, can be particularly challenging for those who stammer. I made it my mission to advocate for more inclusive practices in law schools and courtrooms.

I worked with bar associations to develop guidelines for accommodating lawyers and law students who stammer. These included allowing extra time for oral arguments, permitting written submissions in place of certain oral requirements, and educating judges and opposing counsel about stammering.

One of my proudest achievements was helping to establish a scholarship fund for law students with speech impediments. The fund not only provides financial support but also connects recipients with mentors in the legal profession who have overcome similar challenges.

The Ripple Effect

As my advocacy work continued, I began to see its impact ripple out in unexpected ways. Former mentees became mentors themselves, starting support groups in their law schools or firms. Lawyers who had hidden their stammers for years were inspired to speak openly about their experiences, creating a more inclusive environment for others.

I received letters from people around the world who had seen my TEDx talk or read about my work. They shared their own stories of struggle and triumph, not just with stammering, but with all kinds of personal challenges. It was humbling to realise that by sharing my story, I had given others permission to embrace their own.

One such letter came from a judge in Australia. He wrote about how he had hidden his stammer for decades, fearing it would undermine his authority in the courtroom. After hearing me speak about the power of authenticity, he decided to be open about his stammer. "Your words gave me the courage to be myself," he wrote. "And in doing so, I've become a better judge and a happier person."

Personal Growth Through Advocacy

My journey as an advocate has been as transformative for me as it has been for those I've sought to help. Each time I stand up to speak, each mentoring session, each letter I receive reminds me of the power of turning personal struggle into a force for positive change.

Advocacy has pushed me to continually work on my own speech, not for the sake of achieving perfect fluency, but to be the best communicator I can be. It has challenged me to confront my own lingering insecurities and to practice the self-acceptance I preach to others.

Moreover, it has given me a sense of purpose beyond my legal career. Don't get me wrong – I still love the law and find great fulfillment in my work as an attorney. But advocacy has added a new dimension to my life, allowing me to use my experiences to make a broader impact.

The Ongoing Journey

As I reflect on this chapter of my life, I'm filled with a sense of gratitude and purpose. The journey from a stammering orphan to a successful lawyer was just the beginning. Becoming an advocate has opened up a whole new path, one that I continue to walk with both humility and determination.

There is still much work to be done. Stigma around stammering and other speech impediments persists. Many people still face discrimination and limited opportunities because of how they speak. But I'm heartened by the progress I've seen and the growing community of advocates and allies.

As I prepare for my next speaking engagement, I think about all the voices yet to be heard, all the potential yet to be unlocked. I think about Sarah, now a confident young lawyer, arguing her first real case. I think about Maria, inspiring her classmates with her courage. I think about the judge in Australia, bringing a new level of empathy to his courtroom.

And I'm reminded once again of the power of turning our struggles into strength, of using our experiences to light the way for others. This is the heart of advocacy – not just speaking for others, but empowering them to speak for themselves.

As I step up to the podium, I take a deep breath and smile. The journey continues, and there are still so many stories to be told, so many voices to be amplified. And I'm grateful to play a part in this ongoing narrative of courage, perseverance, and the indomitable human spirit.

Conclusion: The Power of Shared Experiences

As I wrap up this chapter on advocacy, I'm struck by the profound impact of shared experiences. When I first began this journey, I saw my stammer as a deeply personal struggle, something to be overcome in private. But through advocacy, I've learned that our personal challenges, when shared, can become a source of collective strength.

Every time I share my story, whether in a large auditorium or a one-on-one mentoring session, I'm reminded of the universal nature of struggle and resilience. While the specifics may differ, we all face obstacles, we all know the taste of self-doubt, and we all harbour dreams that seem just out of reach.

By opening up about my journey with stammering, I've created a space for others to reflect on their own challenges and aspirations. I've seen how my words can spark recognition in the eyes of a struggling law student, or ignite determination in a child who's been told they can't succeed because of how they speak.

But more importantly, I've learned that advocacy is a two-way street. Every person I've mentored, every audience I've addressed, has taught me something in return. They've shown me new perspectives on resilience, innovative ways to approach challenges, and the incredible diversity of the human experience.

This exchange of experiences and insights is what makes advocacy so powerful. It creates a ripple effect of understanding, empathy, and action that extends far beyond any single individual or cause.

As I look to the future, I'm excited about the possibilities that lie ahead. There are still many barriers to break down, many minds to open, and many voices to amplify. But I'm encouraged by the growing community of advocates and allies I see around me.

To anyone reading this who has ever felt silenced, marginalised, or limited by circumstances beyond their control, I want to say this: Your voice matters. Your experiences, including your struggles, are valuable. And by sharing your story, you have the power to create change, not just for yourself, but for countless others.

As we move forward, let's continue to speak up, to share our stories, and to advocate for a world where everyone's voice is heard and valued. Because in the end, it's not just about overcoming our own challenges – it's about creating a more inclusive, understanding, and empowering world for all.

The journey of advocacy is ongoing, and I'm honoured to be a part of it. Together, we can turn our individual struggles into a collective force for positive change. And in doing so, we can write a new chapter – not just in our own lives, but in the broader story of human progress and understanding.

The High-Profile Case

Taking on a Nationally Recognised Legal Battle

As I stood in front of the mirror, adjusting my tie for what felt like the hundredth time, I couldn't help but reflect on the journey that had led me to this moment. The case that lay before me was unlike anything I had ever faced before. It was a nationally recognised legal battle that would test not only my skills as a lawyer but also my ability to manage my stammer under intense scrutiny.

The case involved a major corporation accused of widespread environmental violations. The implications were far-reaching, potentially affecting thousands of lives and setting a precedent for corporate accountability. As I reviewed the case files one last time, I felt the familiar tightness in my chest, a mixture of excitement and anxiety that I had come to associate with big challenges.

You might wonder how someone who once struggled to say their own name could now be preparing to argue such a high-stakes case. The truth is, I often wondered the same thing. But as I've learned throughout my journey, it's not about eliminating fear or doubt – it's about pushing through them.

I remembered the words of my old speech therapist: "Your voice matters, not just how it sounds." Those words had carried me through many difficult moments, and I clung to them now as I prepared to step into the spotlight.

The courtroom was packed as I made my way to the podium. Cameras flashed, and I could feel the weight of expectation pressing down on me. But as I began to speak, I focused on the techniques I had honed over years of practice. Slow, measured breaths. Visualising the words before speaking them.

Using pauses not as moments of weakness, but as tools to emphasise key points.

As the case unfolded over the following weeks, I found myself drawing on every skill and strategy I had developed throughout my career. There were moments of triumph, like when I successfully cross-examined a key witness, my words flowing smoothly and confidently. And there were moments of struggle, when the pressure caused my stammer to resurface, forcing me to pause and regroup.

But through it all, I remembered that my strength lay not just in my ability to speak, but in my preparation, my understanding of the law, and my dedication to justice.

I had learned long ago that a stammer doesn't define a person's intelligence or capability, and I was determined to prove that on this national stage.

Managing Media Attention with a Stammer

One aspect of the case that I hadn't fully anticipated was the intense media scrutiny. Suddenly, I wasn't just arguing in the courtroom – I was facing cameras and microphones at every turn. Press conferences, interviews, impromptu questions shouted by reporters as I entered or left the courthouse. It was a level of attention I had never experienced before, and it brought with it a whole new set of challenges.

You might think that years of managing my stammer in high-pressure situations would have prepared me for this, but the reality was far more daunting. There's something uniquely stressful about knowing that every word, every pause, every slight stammer could be broadcast to millions of viewers.

I remember the first major press conference. As I approached the podium, I could feel my heart racing. The sea of faces and cameras before me seemed to stretch endlessly. For a moment, I was transported back to my childhood, standing in front of a classroom, paralysed by the fear of speaking.

But then I took a deep breath and reminded myself of how far I had come. I thought of all the people who had supported me along the way – my mentors, my family, even the clients who had put their trust in me despite my speech impediment. I owed it to them, and to myself, to face this challenge head-on.

I began to speak, and to my surprise, I found that the techniques I had developed for the courtroom translated well to this new arena. I used pauses strategically, not just to manage my stammer but to emphasise key points. I maintained eye contact with individual reporters, creating a sense of connection that helped ease my anxiety.

When difficult questions came – and they did – I took my time to formulate responses. I had learned long ago that thoughtful, well-articulated answers were far more valuable than quick, stumbling responses.

And when my stammer did surface, I didn't try to hide it or rush through it. Instead, I acknowledged it with a smile and a brief "Excuse me," before continuing.

Over time, I developed a rapport with many of the regular reporters covering the case. They came to understand and respect my speech patterns, and some even commented on how my openness about my stammer had added a human element to the complex legal proceedings.

It wasn't always easy. There were days when the constant scrutiny felt overwhelming, when a particularly challenging interview left me drained and doubting myself. But I reminded myself that this was part of the journey. Each interaction was an opportunity to show that a person's voice is about much more than just how the words come out.

Proving Capabilities on a Larger Stage

As the case progressed, I found myself not just managing my stammer, but actively using my unique speaking style to my advantage. In the courtroom, I used strategic pauses to build tension and emphasise crucial points. My careful, measured speech pattern lent weight to my arguments, forcing both the judge and jury to lean in and really listen to what I was saying.

Outside the courtroom, my approach to media interactions began to garner attention in its own right. Journalists commented on my ability to distil complex legal concepts into clear, understandable explanations. My unhurried speaking style, born out of necessity, was now being praised for its thoughtfulness and precision.

One particularly memorable moment came during a live television interview. The interviewer, known for his aggressive style, tried to throw me off balance with rapid-fire questions. Instead of becoming flustered, I maintained my composure, taking the time I needed to formulate clear, concise responses. After the interview, I received messages from viewers who appreciated how I had remained calm and articulate under pressure.

As the case neared its conclusion, I found myself reflecting on how far I had come. From a child who struggled to speak in class to a lawyer arguing one of the most high-profile cases in the country. It wasn't just about proving my capabilities as a lawyer – it was about showing that limitations, whether physical or perceived, don't have to define a person's potential.

The day of the final arguments arrived. As I stood before the court, I felt a sense of calm settle over me. I had prepared extensively, not just in terms of the legal arguments, but also in managing my speech. I had practised breathing exercises, visualised a successful outcome, and reminded myself of all the challenges I had overcome to reach this point.

As I began my closing argument, I could feel the eyes of the entire courtroom upon me. But instead of feeling intimidated, I felt empowered. My voice, with its unique rhythm and cadence, filled the room. I spoke of justice, of corporate responsibility, of the lives affected by the actions of the defendant.

There were moments when my stammer surfaced, but I didn't let it derail me. Instead, I incorporated it into my delivery, using the pauses to build emphasis and allow my words to sink in. I could see the jurors leaning forward, hanging on every word.

As I concluded my argument, a hush fell over the courtroom. In that moment, I realised that I had done more than just argue a case – I had shattered preconceptions about what a person with a stammer could achieve.

The verdict, when it came, was in our favour. The corporation was held accountable, setting a precedent that would have far-reaching implications for corporate responsibility. But for me, the victory was about more than just the legal outcome. It was a testament to the power of perseverance, of turning perceived weaknesses into strengths.

In the days that followed, as the media analysed the case and its implications, I found myself fielding questions not just about the legal aspects, but about my personal journey. How had I overcome my stammer to become a successful lawyer? What advice did I have for others facing similar challenges?

These questions gave me pause. My journey had been long and often difficult, filled with moments of doubt and frustration. But it had also been incredibly rewarding. As I considered my responses, I realised that this case had given me a platform to inspire others, to show that with determination and the right support, it's possible to overcome seemingly insurmountable obstacles.

I thought back to the young boy I once was, struggling to speak in class, dreaming of becoming a lawyer but doubting it was possible. If I could speak to that boy now, I would tell him that his voice matters, that his struggles will become his strength, and that one day, he will stand before the world and make a difference – not in spite of his stammer, but because of the resilience and determination it helped him develop.

As this chapter of my career came to a close, I knew that it wasn't an endpoint, but rather a new beginning. The high-profile case had opened doors and created opportunities I had never imagined. But more importantly, it had reinforced a truth I had learned long ago: that our greatest challenges often become our greatest strengths, if we have the courage to face them head-on.

Looking ahead, I felt a renewed sense of purpose. I had proven my capabilities on a larger stage, not just as a lawyer, but as someone who had overcome significant obstacles. Now, I had the opportunity – and the responsibility – to use my experiences to help others find their voice and pursue their dreams, regardless of the challenges they face.

As I prepared for the next phase of my journey, I couldn't help but feel a sense of excitement. The road ahead would undoubtedly have its challenges, but I was ready to face them. After all, every challenge is an opportunity to grow, to learn, and to inspire others. And in that sense, my journey was far from over – it was just beginning.

Chapter 16

Personal Life and Relationships

Navigating Romantic Relationships with a Stammer

As I stood in front of the mirror, adjusting my tie for what felt like the hundredth time, I couldn't help but feel a familiar twinge of anxiety. It wasn't just the usual first-date jitters; it was the nagging worry that had followed me throughout my life: how would my stammer affect this encounter?

You might think that after years of courtroom battles and public speaking engagements, a simple dinner date would be a walk in the park. But the truth is, navigating personal relationships with a speech impediment presents its own unique set of challenges. In the professional world, I had learned to use my stammer as a tool, a way to command attention and respect. But in the realm of romance? That was uncharted territory.

I want to share with you the journey of finding love and building meaningful relationships while managing a stammer. It's a path filled with both heartwarming moments and painful setbacks, but ultimately, it's a story of human connection that transcends the limitations of speech.

The First Hurdle: Making the Ask

For many people with a stammer, the idea of asking someone out on a date can be paralysing. The fear of stumbling over words or being unable to get the question out at all can be overwhelming. I remember the first time I decided to take the plunge and ask out Sarah, a fellow law student I had admired from afar.

I had rehearsed the words countless times in my head: "Would you like to go out for coffee sometime?" Simple enough, right? But as I approached her after class, my heart racing, I felt the familiar tightness in my throat. The words stuck, and I found myself in a moment of panic.

But then something unexpected happened. Sarah, noticing my struggle, smiled encouragingly and said, "Take your time. I'm listening." Her patience and kindness in that moment were a revelation. I managed to get the words out, and to my delight, she said yes.

This experience taught me a valuable lesson: the right person will see beyond the stammer and appreciate you for who you are. It's not about perfect fluency; it's about genuine connection.

Building Trust and Intimacy

As relationships progress, new challenges arise. How do you build intimacy when communication sometimes feels like a struggle? I've found that honesty and vulnerability are key.

In my relationship with Emma, who later became my wife, I made a conscious decision to be open about my stammer from the beginning. On our third date, I explained the nature of my speech impediment, my ongoing efforts to manage it, and how it affected various aspects of my life.

To my surprise, this openness didn't push Emma away. Instead, it brought us closer. She appreciated my candour and began to ask thoughtful questions about my experiences. This dialogue created a foundation of trust and understanding that would prove crucial in our relationship.

For you, dear reader, if you're navigating relationships with a stammer or any other challenge, remember this: your openness invites others to be open in return. It creates a space for genuine connection and mutual understanding.

The Power of Non-Verbal Communication

One of the unexpected benefits of having a stammer is that it forced me to become highly attuned to non-verbal communication. In romantic relationships, this skill proved to be invaluable. I learned to express affection, understanding, and support through touch, facial expressions, and gestures. A gentle squeeze of the hand during a difficult conversation, a knowing look across a crowded room, or a comforting embrace could often convey more than words ever could.

Emma often remarked that she felt more deeply understood in our relationship than she had in previous ones, despite (or perhaps because of) the occasional verbal stumbles. This reminded me that effective communication in relationships goes far beyond just the words we speak.

Building a Family and Support System

The Decision to Start a Family

The decision to start a family is a significant one for any couple, but for someone with a stammer, it comes with additional considerations. Would I be able to read bedtime stories to my children? How would I handle parent-teacher conferences? And perhaps most dauntingly, would my children inherit my stammer?

These were questions that Emma and I grappled with as we contemplated parenthood. We had long, heartfelt discussions about our fears and hopes. Ultimately, we decided that the joy and fulfilment of raising children outweighed our concerns.

When our first child, Lily, was born, I experienced a mix of overwhelming love and anxiety. As I held her in my arms for the first time, I made a silent promise to her: my stammer would never prevent me from being the best father I could be.

Parenting with a Stammer

Parenting, I quickly learned, presented both challenges and unexpected blessings related to my stammer. Reading bedtime stories, something I had worried about, became a cherished nightly ritual. Yes, there were times when I stumbled over words, but Lily never seemed to mind. In fact, as she grew older, she would often giggle and say, "Daddy's doing his special talk!"

I realised that my stammer was teaching my children valuable lessons about patience, perseverance, and accepting differences. They were growing up with a nuanced understanding that communication comes in many forms, and that the content of what you say is far more important than how smoothly you say it.

There were difficult moments too. I remember feeling a pang of sadness when Lily, at age four, asked why some of the other dads at the playground didn't talk like me. But even this became an opportunity for an age-appropriate discussion about diversity and the importance of kindness.

As our family grew with the addition of our son, Max,we found ways to make my stammer a normal, accepted part of our family dynamic. We developed a family motto: "We listen with our hearts." This simple phrase encapsulated our approach to communication, emphasising understanding and patience.

Creating a Support Network

Building a strong support network became crucial as we navigated family life. This network extended beyond just Emma and the children; it included extended family, close friends, and even professional connections who understood and supported my journey.

We cultivated relationships with other families, some of whom had members with various challenges, creating a community of understanding and mutual support. This network became invaluable during times of stress or when we needed advice or simply a listening ear.

I also made sure to stay connected with support groups for people who stammer, both for my own benefit and to be a source of support for others. Sharing experiences with other parents who stammer helped me feel less alone in my journey and provided practical tips for navigating various parenting scenarios.

Balancing Personal Life with a Demanding Career

The Juggling Act

Balancing a high-powered legal career with a rich personal life is challenging for anyone, but adding a stammer to the mix creates an extra layer of complexity. Time management took on a new dimension as I had to factor in speech therapy sessions, practice time for important presentations, and the extra mental energy often required for communication.

I developed a system of prioritisation that allowed me to give my best both at work and at home. This often meant making tough choices. Sometimes, it was declining a high-profile case to ensure I could attend Lily's school play. Other times, it meant missing a family dinner to prepare extensively for a crucial court appearance.

The key, I found, was clear communication with both my family and my colleagues about my needs and limitations. This transparency allowed for greater understanding and flexibility on all sides.

Creating Boundaries

One of the most important lessons I learned was the necessity of creating clear boundaries between work and personal life. This was especially crucial given the extra energy I often expended on managing my speech in professional settings.

I made it a rule to be fully present when I was with my family. This meant no checking work emails during family time and being mentally 'switched off' from work concerns. It wasn't always easy, particularly when a big case was looming, but it was essential for my well-being and for nurturing my relationships.

Emma and I also instituted a weekly 'date night,' a time for us to reconnect amidst the chaos of work and family life. These evenings became a cherished ritual, a reminder of the foundation of our family unit.

The Unexpected Blessings

While balancing career and family life with a stammer presented challenges, it also brought unexpected blessings. My experiences made me a more empathetic lawyer, particularly when dealing with clients who faced communication challenges. This, in turn, enhanced my professional reputation and brought a deeper sense of fulfilment to my work.

At home, my children developed a heightened sense of empathy and understanding. They became natural advocates for inclusion and patience, qualities that their teachers often remarked upon. Seeing these positive traits develop in my children gave me a profound sense of pride and purpose.

Embracing Vulnerability in Relationships

The Strength in Showing Weakness

One of the most transformative realisations in my personal journey was understanding that showing vulnerability, particularly in close relationships, is not a weakness but a strength. For years, I had tried to compensate for my stammer by being extra competent, always in control, never showing any chinks in my armour. But in doing so, I was inadvertently creating distance in my relationships.

It was during a particularly stressful period at work, when I was preparing for a high-stakes trial, that this lesson really hit home. I had been working late nights, pushing myself to the brink of exhaustion. One evening, as I struggled to get through practice for my opening statement, I broke down in frustration.

Emma found me in my home office, tears of anger and exhaustion streaming down my face. Instead of trying to hide my moment of weakness, I allowed myself to be vulnerable. I shared my fears about the case, my worries about letting people down, and the exhaustion I felt from constantly managing my speech.

That moment of raw honesty brought us closer than ever before. Emma's support and understanding gave me strength, and I realised that by allowing her to see my struggles, I was giving her the opportunity to be there for me in a meaningful way.

This experience taught me to be more open about my challenges, not just with Emma, but with my children and close friends as well. It deepened our connections and created a home environment where everyone felt safe to express their own vulnerabilities.

Navigating Conflict with a Stammer

Conflict is an inevitable part of any relationship, but when you have a stammer, it can present unique challenges. In the heat of an argument, when emotions are running high, managing speech can become even more difficult.

Early in our marriage, Emma and I struggled with this. During disagreements, my stammer would often worsen, leading to frustration on both sides. I felt unheard and misunderstood, while Emma felt that I was shutting down or withholding.

We realised we needed to develop strategies to navigate conflict in a way that worked for both of us. We established a 'timeout' signal, which either of us could use when things got too heated. This gave me time to collect my thoughts and manage my speech, and it gave both of us a chance to cool down.

We also adopted a practice of writing down our thoughts during conflicts. This allowed me to express myself fully without the pressure of immediate verbal response, and it gave Emma insight into my perspective that might have been lost in the struggle of verbal communication.

These strategies not only helped us resolve conflicts more effectively but also deepened our understanding of each other's communication needs and styles.

Teaching Children About Difference and Acceptance

As a parent with a stammer, I had a unique opportunity to teach my children about difference, acceptance, and the many forms that communication can take. From an early age, we engaged in open, age-appropriate discussions about my stammer and what it meant.

We read books about diversity and different ways of speaking. We practised active listening skills as a family, emphasising the importance of focusing on the content of what someone is saying rather than how they're saying it.

As the children grew older, we encouraged them to be advocates for acceptance in their own social circles. I remember feeling immensely proud when Lily, then in second grade, told me about standing up for a classmate who was being teased for his lisp.

These ongoing conversations and experiences shaped our children's worldview, fostering empathy and inclusivity that extended far beyond just understanding speech differences.

The Role of Humour in Relationships

Laughing at Ourselves

One of the most powerful tools I've found in navigating relationships with a stammer is humour. Learning to laugh at myself and finding the lighter side of challenging situations has been incredibly liberating, both for me and for those around me.

I remember a family dinner where I was struggling particularly hard with a word. After several attempts, I finally got it out, only to realise I'd forgotten what I was talking about in the first place. Instead of feeling embarrassed, I laughed and said, "Well, I hope that word was worth the wait!" The whole family joined in the laughter, and what could have been an awkward moment became a shared, joyful one.

This ability to find humour in difficult situations has been a cornerstone of my relationship with Emma. It's diffused tension, created bonds, and reminded us not to take everything so seriously. More importantly, it's shown our children that it's okay to laugh at yourself sometimes, and that challenges don't have to define or limit you.

Creating Inside Jokes

Over the years, Emma and I have developed a repertoire of inside jokes related to my stammer. These shared moments of humour have become a special part of our relationship, a private language that strengthens our bond.

For instance, whenever I have a particularly smooth day of speaking, Emma will jokingly ask, "Who are you and what have you done with my husband?" Or when I'm struggling with a word, she'll playfully offer ridiculous alternatives, turning a potentially frustrating moment into a game.

These moments of levity have been crucial in maintaining a positive outlook, even during challenging times. They've reminded us to find joy in our journey together, stammer and all.

Redefining Success in Personal Relationships

Beyond Words: Connection and Understanding

As I've navigated personal relationships with a stammer, I've had to redefine what success looks like. In a world that often values quick, articulate speech, I've learned that true connection goes far beyond words.

Success in relationships, I've found, is about creating a deep understanding and emotional bond. It's about being truly present with your loved ones, listening actively, and showing care through actions as well as words.

With Emma, success is the comfort of silent understanding we've developed over the years. It's the way she can read my mood from the slightest change in my expression, and how I can sense her needs often before she expresses them.

With my children, success is the trust and openness we've cultivated. It's seeing them grow into empathetic, patient individuals who value people for who they are, not how they speak.

Celebrating Small Victories

Another important aspect of redefining success has been learning to celebrate small victories. In the context of my stammer, this might mean acknowledging a smooth conversation with a new acquaintance, or successfully giving a speech at a family event.

We've made it a family practice to celebrate these moments, not because they represent a 'victory' over my stammer, but because they represent courage, perseverance, and growth. This practice has extended beyond just my speech-related achievements, creating a family culture where we all celebrate each other's small steps forward.

The Ripple Effect of Authenticity

Perhaps the most profound realisation I've had about success in personal relationships is the power of authenticity. By embracing my stammer as part of who I am, rather than something to be hidden or overcome, I've created space for genuine connections.

This authenticity has had a ripple effect, encouraging those around me to be more open about their own challenges and insecurities. I've watched Emma become more comfortable expressing her own vulnerabilities, and I've seen our children develop a remarkable capacity for empathy and acceptance of others.

In this way, what once seemed like a barrier to connection has become a catalyst for deeper, more meaningful relationships. My stammer, rather than limiting my personal life, has enriched it in ways I never could have imagined.

Looking Ahead: Continued Growth and Learning

Embracing Lifelong Learning

As I reflect on my journey of navigating personal relationships with a stammer, I'm struck by how much I continue to learn and grow. Each new phase of life brings new challenges and opportunities for growth.

As our children enter their teenage years, we're navigating new territories of communication and understanding. I'm learning to adapt my parenting style, finding ways to connect with them that respect their growing independence while still providing the support and guidance they need.

In my relationship with Emma, we continue to evolve and discover new depths to our connection. We've started taking couples' communication workshops together, not because we're struggling, but because we believe in continually investing in and strengthening our relationship.

Paying It Forward

One of the most rewarding aspects of my journey has been the opportunity to support others who are navigating similar challenges. Emma and I have become mentors to other couples where one partner has a stammer or another communication challenge.

We've also started a support group for parents with speech impediments, creating a space where we can share experiences, offer advice, and provide encouragement. Seeing others find hope and strength in our story has been incredibly fulfilling and has given new meaning to our own experiences.

Embracing the Unknown

As I look to the future, I'm filled with a sense of excitement and curiosity. I know there will be new challenges to face - perhaps as we become grandparents one day, or as we navigate the later stages of our careers and eventually retirement. But I face these unknowns with confidence, knowing that the skills and resilience we've developed will serve us well. More importantly, I know that whatever comes our way, we'll face it together, with patience, understanding, and love.

Conclusion: Love Beyond Words

As we conclude this chapter on personal life and relationships, I want to leave you with this thought: love, in its truest form, transcends the limitations of speech. It resides in the silent understanding between partners, in the patient listening of a child, in the supportive network of family and friends who see beyond the surface to the person within.

My journey with a stammer has taught me that the most profound connections are often forged not in perfect fluency, but in moments of vulnerability, authenticity, and shared understanding. It has shown me that our challenges, when embraced and shared openly, can become the very things that bring us closer to those we love.

To you, dear reader, whether you stammer or not, I encourage you to approach your relationships with openness, patience, and a willingness to look beyond words. Cultivate understanding, celebrate differences, and remember that true connection often happens in the spaces between words.

As we move forward into the next chapter, where we'll explore how these personal experiences have shaped my approach to giving back to the community, remember this: every challenge you face in your personal life is an opportunity for growth, deeper connection, and ultimately, a richer, more authentic way of being in the world.

Chapter 17

Giving Back

Establishing a Foundation for Speech Therapy Support

As I stood at the podium, looking out over the sea of expectant faces, I couldn't help but reflect on how far I'd come. Just a few decades ago, the very thought of public speaking would have sent me into a spiral of anxiety and self-doubt. Now, here I was, about to announce the launch of a foundation that would change the lives of countless individuals struggling with speech impediments.

"Welcome, everyone," I began, my voice steady and clear. "Today marks the beginning of a new chapter in our collective journey to empower those with speech disorders."

The journey to this moment had been long and, at times, arduous. After years of personal struggle and professional success, I had finally reached a point where I could give back in a meaningful way. The idea for the foundation had been brewing for some time, born from a deep-seated desire to help others overcome the challenges I had faced.

You see, throughout my career, I had encountered many young people who reminded me of my younger self – bright, ambitious, but held back by the invisible chains of a stutter or other speech impediment.

Their stories resonated with me, stirring memories of my own battles and triumphs. It was then that I realised I had a unique opportunity – and perhaps even a responsibility – to use my experiences and resources to make a difference.

The foundation's primary goal was to provide accessible, high-quality speech therapy to those who might otherwise not be able to afford it. I remembered all too well the transformative impact that speech therapy had had on my own life, and I wanted to ensure that others had the same opportunity.

"Our mission," I continued, my voice growing stronger with each word, "is to break down the barriers that prevent individuals from accessing the support they need. We will fund speech therapy programmes, sponsor research into innovative treatment methods, and provide scholarships for aspiring speech-language pathologists."

As I spoke, I could see the excitement building in the audience. There were nods of agreement, smiles of encouragement, and even a few tears. I knew that many in attendance had their own stories of struggle with speech disorders, either personally or through loved ones. Their support and enthusiasm fuelled my determination to make this foundation a success.

Organising Workshops and Seminars for Stutterers

With the foundation established, our next step was to create a comprehensive programme of workshops and seminars designed specifically for individuals who stutter. I wanted to go beyond traditional speech therapy and provide a holistic approach that addressed not just the physical aspects of stuttering, but also the emotional and psychological impacts.

Our first workshop was held in a small community centre, with about twenty participants ranging in age from teenagers to seniors. As I walked into the room, I could feel the nervous energy palpable in the air. It reminded me of my own anxiety in similar situations years ago.

"Good morning, everyone," I said, making eye contact with each participant. "I want you to know that this is a safe space. Here, we're all on the same journey, and there's no judgement, only support and understanding."

I shared my own story, not holding back on the challenges and setbacks I had faced. As I spoke, I could see the tension in the room begin to dissipate. Shoulders relaxed, faces softened, and a few brave souls even managed small smiles.

The workshop covered a range of topics, from practical speech techniques to strategies for managing anxiety in social situations. We brought in expert speech therapists, psychologists, and even a yoga instructor to teach relaxation techniques. But perhaps the most powerful moments were during the group discussions, where participants could share their experiences and offer support to one another.

One young woman, Sarah, stood up towards the end of the day. Her voice quivered as she began to speak, but she persevered. "I've never been in a room with so many people who understand," she said, tears glistening in her eyes. "For the first time, I don't feel alone."

Her words struck a chord with everyone in the room, myself included. It was a poignant reminder of why we had started this foundation in the first place – to create a community where people like Sarah could find understanding, support, and hope.

As the workshops and seminars grew in popularity, we expanded our reach. We began offering online sessions for those who couldn't attend in person, and we developed specialised programmes for different age groups and specific types of speech disorders. Each new initiative brought its own challenges, but seeing the positive impact on participants made every effort worthwhile.

Becoming an Inspiration in the Legal and Disability Communities

While the foundation's work was incredibly fulfilling, I found myself being called upon to share my story in broader contexts. Law firms, disability advocacy groups, and even corporations began inviting me to speak about my journey from a stuttering orphan to a successful lawyer and advocate.

At first, I was hesitant. Despite my years of public speaking experience in the courtroom, the idea of talking about my personal struggles still made me uncomfortable. But I realised that by sharing my story, I could potentially inspire others facing similar challenges.

One particular speaking engagement stands out in my memory. It was at a large law school, where I had been invited to give a keynote address to the incoming class. As I stood on the stage, looking out at the sea of eager young faces, I was transported back to my own law school days.

"When I was sitting where you are now," I began, "I was terrified. Not just of the challenging coursework or the competitive environment, but of the simple act of speaking up in class. You see, I have a stutter."

I paused, letting my words sink in. I could see the surprise on some faces, the curiosity on others.

"But here's what I want you to understand," I continued. "Your challenges, whatever they may be, do not define you. They are not limitations, but opportunities for growth. They are the fire that can forge you into something stronger, more resilient, and more empathetic."

As I shared my journey – the struggles, the setbacks, and the eventual triumphs – I could see the impact my words were having. There were nods of understanding, looks of admiration, and even a few tears.

After the speech, a young man approached me. He introduced himself as Alex and shared that he too had a stutter. "I was thinking of dropping out," he admitted. "I didn't think I could make it as a lawyer with my speech impediment. But hearing your story... it's given me hope."

Moments like these reinforced the importance of visibility and representation. By standing up and sharing our stories, we not only inspire others facing similar challenges but also educate those who might not understand the struggles of living with a disability.

My advocacy work extended beyond the legal community. I began collaborating with disability rights organisations, lending my voice and legal expertise to their causes. We worked on initiatives to improve accessibility in public spaces, fight discrimination in the workplace, and promote inclusive education policies.

One project I'm particularly proud of is a mentorship programme we established, pairing successful professionals who have overcome speech disorders with young people facing similar challenges. The programme has not only provided practical support and guidance but has also helped to build a network of understanding and encouragement that extends far beyond the legal profession.

As my profile in the disability community grew, I found myself increasingly called upon to comment on relevant issues in the media. It was a role I approached with both excitement and trepidation. On one hand, it was an opportunity to bring important issues to the forefront of public discourse. On the other, it meant exposing myself – and my stutter – to a much wider audience.

I remember my first live television interview vividly. As the makeup artist applied the final touches and the producer counted down to airtime, I felt the familiar tightness in my chest that often preceded a stutter. But I took a deep breath, reminding myself of how far I'd come and of all the people I was representing.

"Welcome to the programme," the host began. "We're joined today by a prominent lawyer and disability rights advocate to discuss recent legislation affecting individuals with speech disorders."

As I began to speak, I could feel my stutter threatening to emerge. But instead of fighting it, I acknowledged it openly. "As someone who has lived with a stutter all my life," I said, pausing to navigate a difficult sound, "I can attest to the importance of this legislation."

The host, to her credit, gave me the time I needed to express my thoughts. And as the interview progressed, I found my rhythm, articulating the key points with clarity and passion.

After the interview, my phone was flooded with messages of support and encouragement. But the one that touched me most was from a parent who wrote, "My son, who stutters, saw you on TV today. He turned to me and said, 'Dad, if he can do it, so can I.' Thank you for being a role model."

It was moments like these that reinforced the importance of visibility and representation. By putting myself out there, stutters and all, I was showing others that it was possible to succeed not in spite of their challenges, but because of the strength and resilience those challenges had helped them develop.

As I reflect on this chapter of my life – the foundation, the workshops, the speaking engagements – I'm filled with a sense of purpose and gratitude. The journey from a stuttering orphan to a successful lawyer was not an easy one, but it has equipped me with the tools and experiences to make a real difference in the lives of others.

Every time I stand in front of a group of stutterers at a workshop, or address a room full of law students, or speak out on disability rights in the media, I'm reminded of the power of perseverance and the importance of giving back. It's not always easy, and there are still days when my stutter gets the better of me. But I've learned that it's not about being perfect – it's about being present, being authentic, and being willing to use your voice, however it may sound, to make a positive impact in the world.

As we continue to grow our initiatives and reach more people, I'm excited about the future. There's still so much work to be done, so many lives to touch, so many barriers to break down. But with each person we help, each story we share, and each mind we open, we're creating a world that's a little more understanding, a little more inclusive, and a lot more compassionate.

And to you, dear reader, whether you're facing your own challenges with speech or any other obstacle in life, I want you to know this: Your voice matters. Your story is important. And you have the power to turn your struggles into strength, not just for yourself, but for others who may be walking a similar path.

So speak up, even if your voice shakes. Stand tall, even if your knees are trembling. And never, ever let anyone tell you that you can't achieve your dreams. Because if there's one thing I've learned on this journey, it's that our greatest limitations are often the ones we place on ourselves. Break free from those self-imposed constraints, and you'll be amazed at what you can achieve.

As we close this chapter and look ahead to the next, remember that every end is just a new beginning. The work of giving back, of making a difference, is never truly finished. There will always be new challenges to face, new battles to fight, and new lives to touch. But with perseverance, compassion, and the support of a community that understands, there's no limit to what we can accomplish.

So let's continue this journey together, supporting each other, inspiring change, and proving that even the most challenging obstacles can be overcome. After all, it's not just about our own success – it's about paving the way for others to follow, creating a world where everyone's voice can be heard, regardless of how it may sound.

Chapter 18

The Landmark Judgement

A Case That Changed Everything

As I stood before the Supreme Court, my heart raced with a mixture of anticipation and nervousness. This wasn't just any case; it was the culmination of my lifelong journey, a chance to make a real difference in the legal world. The case before us had the potential to change legal precedent, and I knew that every word I spoke would carry immense weight.

You might wonder how someone who once struggled to say their own name could now be arguing a landmark case in the highest court of the land. The journey has been long and challenging, but each step has led me to this moment.

Preparing for the Battle of a Lifetime

The weeks leading up to the hearing were a whirlwind of preparation. My team and I worked tirelessly, poring over legal documents, precedents, and expert testimonies. We knew that this case could set a new standard for civil rights, and the responsibility weighed heavily on our shoulders.

As I rehearsed my arguments, I couldn't help but reflect on how far I'd come. There was a time when the thought of speaking in public would have paralysed me with fear. Now, here I was, ready to address the most important audience of my career.

The Morning of Reckoning

On the morning of the hearing, I woke up before dawn. The familiar knot of anxiety in my stomach was there, but it was different now. It was no longer debilitating; instead, it fuelled my determination. I went through my usual routine – deep breathing exercises, vocal warm-ups, and a final review of my notes.

As I put on my best suit, I caught a glimpse of myself in the mirror. The face looking back at me was no longer that of a scared, stammering boy, but of a confident, accomplished lawyer. I smiled, knowing that regardless of the outcome, I had already won my personal battle.

Walking into History

The Supreme Court building loomed before me, its marble columns a testament to the enduring nature of justice. As I climbed the steps, I thought of all the great legal minds who had walked this path before me. Now, it was my turn to leave my mark.

Inside, the atmosphere was charged with anticipation. I could feel the eyes of my colleagues, the opposing counsel, and the justices upon me. In that moment, I made a conscious decision to embrace my journey, stammer and all. It was part of who I was, and it had shaped me into the advocate I had become.

The Case Begins

As the Chief Justice called the court to order, a hush fell over the room. I took my place at the podium, my hands steady as I arranged my notes. When I began to speak, my voice was clear and strong. The occasional stutter that punctuated my speech no longer felt like a weakness; it was a reminder of the obstacles I had overcome.

"May it please the court," I began, my words measured and deliberate. "We stand before you today to argue a case that strikes at the very heart of our nation's commitment to equality and justice."

As I delved into the details of the case, I could see the justices leaning in, their expressions intent. They asked probing questions, challenging our arguments, but I was prepared. Years of managing my stammer had taught me the value of careful consideration before speaking, and this skill now served me well in crafting precise, thoughtful responses.

A Moment of Truth

Midway through my argument, I encountered a particularly challenging question from one of the justices. In the past, such moments might have triggered a severe stammer, leaving me struggling for words. But as I took a deep breath, I felt a sense of calm wash over me.

"Your Honour," I said, my voice steady, "The crux of this issue lies not in the letter of the law, but in its spirit." I paused, allowing the weight of my words to sink in. "We must ask ourselves: does our current interpretation truly serve justice, or does it perpetuate the very inequalities our Constitution seeks to prevent?"

As I continued, I could see a shift in the room. The justices leaned forward, their pens scribbling furiously. Even the opposing counsel seemed to be listening with renewed interest. In that moment, I knew that regardless of the outcome, we had succeeded in making them think, in challenging the status quo.

The Power of Perseverance

As I neared the end of my argument, I felt a surge of emotion. This case represented not just a legal battle, but a personal triumph. Every stammer, every moment of doubt, every obstacle I had faced had led me to this moment.

"Your Honours," I said, my voice resonating through the chamber, "we stand at a crossroads. The decision you make today will echo through the annals of legal history. It will determine whether we, as a nation, choose to move forward towards greater equality and justice, or whether we remain tethered to outdated interpretations that no longer serve our evolving society."

As I delivered my closing remarks, I felt a sense of clarity and purpose that I had never experienced before. The words flowed seamlessly, my argument building to a powerful crescendo. In that moment, I wasn't just a lawyer arguing a case; I was a voice for countless individuals who had been silenced by injustice.

The Waiting Game

With my argument concluded, all that was left was to wait. The days that followed were a blur of media interviews, discussions with my team, and anxious anticipation. As we waited for the court's decision, I found myself reflecting on the journey that had brought me here.

I thought of the young boy who once struggled to speak his own name, of the countless nights spent practicing in front of a mirror, of the teachers and mentors who had believed in me when I couldn't believe in myself. Each memory was a testament to the power of perseverance, a reminder that our greatest obstacles can become our greatest strengths.

The Verdict

When the day of the decision finally arrived, the tension was palpable. As the Chief Justice began to read the opinion, I held my breath, my heart pounding in my chest.

"In a 7-2 decision, the court rules in favour of the plaintiff..."

The rest of the words faded into a blur as the realisation sank in. We had won. The landmark judgement we had fought so hard for was now a reality. As the implications of the decision began to sink in, I felt a wave of emotion wash over me.

This wasn't just a victory for our clients or our legal team. It was a victory for every person who had ever felt marginalised or silenced. It was proof that one voice, no matter how challenged, could make a difference.

The Aftermath

In the days that followed, the impact of the decision began to unfold. Legal experts hailed it as a game-changer, predicting far-reaching implications for civil rights cases across the country. Media outlets clamoured for interviews, eager to hear from the lawyer who had argued the landmark case.

As I sat in countless interviews, I made a conscious decision to speak openly about my journey. I wanted people to understand that this victory wasn't just about legal expertise; it was about the triumph of the human spirit over adversity.

"This case," I told one reporter, "is proof that our perceived weaknesses can become our greatest strengths. My stammer taught me the power of careful, thoughtful communication. It taught me to listen, to consider my words carefully, and to speak with purpose and conviction."

Reflections on a Journey

In the quiet moments between the flurry of activity, I found myself reflecting on the long road that had led me here. I thought of the young boy who once believed his stammer would forever hold him back, who couldn't imagine a future where his voice would be heard and respected.

If I could speak to that boy now, I would tell him that his struggles are not in vain. That every moment of frustration, every tear of disappointment, is shaping him into the advocate he is meant to become. I would tell him that his stammer is not a weakness to be overcome, but a unique perspective that will one day allow him to connect with and fight for those who have been silenced.

A New Chapter Begins

As the dust settled and the impact of the landmark judgement began to take shape, I realised that this was not an endpoint, but a new beginning. The case had opened doors and created opportunities I had never imagined possible.

Invitations poured in from law schools, asking me to speak about the case and my journey. Civil rights organisations reached out, seeking collaboration on new initiatives. Even my own law firm was evolving, with a renewed focus on taking on cases that could make a real difference in people's lives.

Paying It Forward

In the midst of this whirlwind, I made a decision. It was time to use this platform, this moment in the spotlight, to give back in a meaningful way. I reached out to organisations that support individuals with speech impediments, offering to share my story and provide mentorship.

I remembered the impact that my first supportive teacher had on my life, how that one person who believed in me had changed everything. Now, I had the opportunity to be that person for others.

The Power of One Voice

As I stand here now, looking back on this landmark case and all that has followed, I am filled with a sense of awe and gratitude. I am in awe of the power of the human spirit to overcome seemingly insurmountable obstacles. I am grateful for every person who supported me on this journey, who saw potential where others saw limitation.

But most of all, I am struck by the realisation that one voice – even a stammering one – can change the world. This case, this moment in history, is proof that our words have power, that our stories matter, and that our perceived weaknesses can become our greatest strengths.

A Message to You, Dear Reader

As I conclude this chapter, I want to speak directly to you, dear reader. Perhaps you are facing your own obstacles, battling your own demons. Maybe you, too, have a voice inside you that longs to be heard but is held back by fear or doubt.

To you, I say this: Your voice matters. Your story is important. The very things that you believe holds you back may be the source of your greatest strength. Embrace your journey, with all its challenges and triumphs. For it is through these experiences that you will find your true voice, your unique perspective that the world desperately needs.

Remember, the path to success is rarely smooth or straight. It is a winding road, full of detours and obstacles. But each challenge you face, each obstacle you overcome, is shaping you into the person you are meant to become.

So, speak up, even if your voice shakes. Stand tall, even when the world tries to push you down. For you never know – your words, your actions, your very presence might just change the course of history.

As we move forward from this landmark judgement, I am filled with hope and excitement for what the future holds. For myself, for the legal profession, and for every individual who has ever felt silenced or marginalised. This case has shown us that change is possible, that justice can prevail, and that every voice deserves to be heard.

And so, we forge ahead, ready to take on the next challenge, to fight the next battle. For in the end, it is not just about winning cases or changing laws. It's about changing lives, one voice at a time.

Chapter 19

Reflections on an Unspoken Journey

Looking Back on Challenges Overcome

As I sit here, pen in hand, reflecting on the journey that has brought me to this point, I'm overwhelmed by a sense of gratitude and awe. You, dear reader, have walked with me through the pages of this book.

witnessing the struggles, triumphs, and everything in between. Now, let's take a moment to look back on the challenges we've overcome together.

Remember that young orphan boy, struggling to form even the simplest of sentences? That was me, a child whose world had been shattered by loss and whose voice was trapped behind an unyielding stammer. I can still feel the ache in my chest when I think about those early days – the frustration, the isolation, the burning desire to be understood.

You've seen how that boy faced ridicule in the classroom, how he spent countless silent nights wrestling with self-doubt and fear. But you've also witnessed his determination, the seed of resilience that took root and grew stronger with each passing year.

I want you to know that your own challenges, whatever they may be, are not insurmountable. Just as I found my way through the maze of stuttering, you too can navigate the obstacles in your path. It's not about being fearless; it's about facing your fears head-on and refusing to let them define you.

The Power of Perseverance

One of the most crucial lessons I've learned on this journey is the immense power of perseverance. There were countless moments when giving up seemed like the easiest option – when the stares became too much to bear, when the words refused to come, when the dream of becoming a lawyer seemed like a cruel joke.

But here's the thing about perseverance: it's not about never falling; it's about always getting back up. Every time I stumbled, every time I felt like I couldn't go on, I reminded myself of the reasons why I started this journey in the first place. I thought about the young boy who dreamed of standing in a courtroom, fighting for justice. I thought about all the other people out there struggling with speech impediments, needing someone to show them that it's possible to overcome.

You, too, have that strength within you. Whatever challenges you're facing, remember that every setback is an opportunity for a comeback. Perseverance isn't just about gritting your teeth and pushing through; it's about finding creative solutions, adapting your approach, and never losing sight of your ultimate goal.

The Transformative Power of Support

As I look back on my journey, I'm struck by the profound impact that support and mentorship have had on my life. From that first supportive teacher who saw beyond my stammer to the allies and mentors who guided me through college and law school, I've been blessed with people who believed in me even when I struggled to believe in myself.

I want you to know that you don't have to face your challenges alone. Reach out, be vulnerable, and allow others to support you. Sometimes, the simple act of sharing your struggles can lighten the load and open doors you never knew existed.

Remember the chapter where we talked about building a support network? That network has been my lifeline, my source of strength when things get tough. Whether it was my family, my mentors in the legal profession, or the stuttering community, I've learned that there's immense power in connection and shared experiences.

If you're facing a challenge that seems insurmountable, I encourage you to seek out others who have walked a similar path. Their insights, their understanding, and their support can be transformative. And as you grow and overcome your own obstacles, don't forget to pay it forward. Be that supportive voice for someone else who's struggling.

Turning Weaknesses into Strengths

One of the most profound realisations I've had on this journey is that our perceived weaknesses can often become our greatest strengths. My stammer, which I once saw as nothing but a hindrance, has shaped me in ways I never could have imagined.

It taught me patience – with myself and with others. It honed my ability to listen, to truly hear what others are saying beyond just their words. It made me more empathetic, more attuned to the struggles of those around me. And perhaps most importantly, it taught me the power of perseverance and the sweet taste of overcoming seemingly insurmountable odds.

I want you to look at your own perceived weaknesses or challenges. How have they shaped you? What strengths have they cultivated within you? Perhaps a physical limitation has made you more resourceful. Maybe a learning difficulty has enhanced your problem-solving skills. Or like me, perhaps a communication challenge has deepened your capacity for empathy and understanding.

Don't shy away from your struggles or try to hide them. Embrace them, learn from them, and let them fuel your growth. You'll be amazed at how these very challenges can become the cornerstone of your success.

The Journey of Self-Acceptance

Throughout this book, we've talked a lot about overcoming obstacles and achieving success. But one of the most important lessons I've learned – and one that I hope you'll take to heart – is the importance of self-acceptance.

For years, I saw my stammer as something to be conquered, an enemy to be vanquished. I pushed myself relentlessly, always striving for perfection in my speech.

But true freedom came when I learned to accept myself, stammer and all.

This doesn't mean giving up or resigning yourself to limitations. Rather, it's about acknowledging your whole self – strengths, weaknesses, quirks, and all – and recognising your inherent worth beyond any single characteristic or challenge.

I remember the day I stood in front of a mirror and said, out loud and with all my stammers, "I am enough." It was a turning point. From that moment on, my energy shifted from fighting against myself to working with myself, the stammer was part of me, but it didn't define me.

I encourage you to practice this self-acceptance in your own life. Whatever challenge you're facing, whatever aspect of yourself you're struggling with, try saying out loud: "This is part of me, but it doesn't define me. I am enough."

The Power of Representation

As my career progressed and I found myself in more high-profile cases, I became acutely aware of the power of representation. Every time I stood up in court, every time I spoke at a conference or gave an interview, I was not just representing myself or my clients. I was representing every person who had ever felt marginalised because of a speech impediment or any other perceived difference.

This realisation was both a responsibility and a source of strength. It pushed me to excel, to show the world that a stammer was no barrier to success in even the most communication-intensive professions.

But more than that, it opened my eyes to the importance of diversity in all fields. When we allow diverse voices to be heard – whether they stammer, speak with an accent, or communicate in entirely different ways – we enrich our collective understanding and create a more inclusive world.

I encourage you to think about how you can be a representative for others who might be facing similar challenges. Your success, your visibility, your voice – however it sounds – can be a beacon of hope and a catalyst for change.

Balancing Professional Success and Personal Growth

As we've journeyed through the chapters of this book, you've seen how my professional life evolved – from struggling student to respected advocate, from small cases to nationally recognised legal battles. But alongside this professional growth, there was an equally important personal journey.

Learning to navigate romantic relationships with a stammer, building a family, finding balance between a demanding career and a fulfilling personal life – these were challenges that required just as much courage and perseverance as any courtroom battle.

I want you to know that success is not just about professional achievements. True success encompasses all aspects of life – relationships, personal growth, emotional well-being, and giving back to others. As you pursue your own goals, remember to nurture all parts of yourself.

For me, this meant learning to be vulnerable in my personal relationships, allowing my loved ones to see and accept all parts of me, stammer included. It meant setting boundaries to ensure I had time for family, for self-care, for the simple joys of life outside of work.

It also meant recognising that my journey wasn't just about me. As I grew more successful, I felt a growing responsibility to give back, to use my experiences to help others facing similar challenges. This led to the creation of my foundation for speech therapy support and the workshops for young stutterers.

I encourage you to think holistically about your own success. How can you balance your professional goals with personal growth? How can you use your experiences to uplift others?

The Ongoing Nature of Growth

As we near the end of this chapter – and this book – I want to emphasise that growth and learning are ongoing processes. Even now, decades into my career, with numerous legal victories under my belt and a stable personal life, I'm still learning, still growing, still facing new challenges.

The landmark judgement we discussed in the previous chapter was a pinnacle of my career, a moment when I delivered a powerful, stammer-free closing argument that changed legal precedent. But it wasn't an endpoint. Rather, it was another step in an ongoing journey.

I still have days when my stammer reasserts itself. I still face moments of self-doubt. But now, I have the tools, the support, and the self-awareness to navigate these challenges. More importantly, I have the perspective to see them as opportunities for further growth rather than setbacks.

I want you to carry this mindset with you as you face your own challenges. Every obstacle is an opportunity to learn, every setback a chance to come back stronger. Your journey doesn't end when you achieve a goal or overcome a particular challenge. It's a lifelong process of growth, learning, and becoming more fully yourself.

Insights Gained and Lessons Learned

As I reflect on this unspoken journey, there are several key insights I want to share with you:

1. **Authenticity is power**: For years, I tried to hide my stammer, to be someone I wasn't. But true strength came when I learned to be authentically myself, stammer and all. Whatever your challenge, don't waste energy trying to be someone else. Your authentic self is your most powerful self.

2. **Resilience is a muscle**: The more you face your fears and push through challenges, the stronger your resilience becomes. Every time you choose to persevere, you're building that muscle.

3. **Communication is more than words**: My stammer taught me that effective communication goes far beyond verbal fluency. Body language, empathy, active listening – these are all crucial components of truly connecting with others.

4. **Success is personal**: Don't let others define success for you. For me, success wasn't just about winning cases or gaining recognition. It was about personal growth, making a difference in others' lives, and finding inner peace with my stammer.

5. **Support is crucial**: No one achieves anything alone. Build your support network, and don't be afraid to lean on it when you need to.

6. **Giving back enriches your own journey**: Some of my most fulfilling experiences have come from mentoring others and advocating for the stuttering community. Your challenges give you unique insights – use them to help others.

7. **Growth is a lifelong journey**: There's no final destination where all your problems are solved. Embrace the ongoing nature of personal growth and learning.

8. **Your challenges can become your strengths**: The very things that seem like obstacles can often become your greatest assets. My stammer made me a more empathetic, patient, and determined person.

A Message of Hope and Perseverance

As we come to the close of this chapter and this book, I want to leave you with a message of hope. Whatever challenges you're facing, whatever obstacles seem insurmountable, I want you to know that you have the strength within you to overcome them.

Your journey may not look like mine. Your challenges may be different, your path unique. But the principles of perseverance, self-acceptance, and growth apply universally.

Remember the stuttering orphan boy we met at the beginning of this book? He never could have imagined the life that lay ahead of him. The courtroom victories, the lives touched, the personal growth and fulfilment – all of it seemed impossible from where he stood.

But step by step, day by day, with determination, support, and a willingness to keep pushing forward, that boy found his voice. He turned his greatest challenge into his greatest strength. He built a life and a career that once seemed like an impossible dream.

You have that same potential within you. Your voice matters, whether it comes out fluently or with a stammer, whether it's spoken aloud or expressed in other ways. Your struggles do not define you, but they can refine you, shaping you into a stronger, more compassionate, more resilient version of yourself.

As you close this book and continue on your own journey, I want you to carry with you the knowledge that you are capable of more than you know. Your challenges do not limit you – they are the forge in which your strength is tempered.

So, step forward boldly. Face your fears. Embrace your authentic self. Build your support network. And never, never give up on your dreams. Your unspoken courage is waiting to be discovered, and your journey of growth and self-discovery is just beginning.

Remember, every great story of success and perseverance starts with a single step. You've taken that step by reading this book. Now, it's time to write your own story of unspoken courage. I believe in you, and I can't wait to see where your journey takes you.

As we close the final chapter of Jake's journey with the magical money, I hope you've found yourself as transformed as our young protagonist. Remember when we first met Jake, stumbling upon that mysterious torn note? Like him, you may have wondered what you'd do with such power. But through Jake's adventures, we've learned that true magic lies not in the money itself, but in how we choose to use it.

Throughout this book, we've explored the challenges and temptations that come with unexpected power. From helping the homeless man to resisting the allure of the toy store, Jake's experiences mirror our own daily struggles with empathy, generosity, and self-control. I bet you've faced similar dilemmas in your own life, haven't you? It's not always easy to make the right choice, but Jake's journey shows us that it's always worth it.

The lessons Jake learned about loyalty, problem-solving, and conflict resolution are timeless. Remember how he helped his friend without revealing the note's secret? Or how he chose a positive solution when confronted by the bully? These moments remind us that true strength comes from within, not from external sources of power. I've found myself in similar situations, and I can tell you, the satisfaction of doing the right thing far outweighs any temporary gain from taking the easy way out.

As Jake discovered the joy of selfless giving at the community fair, I hope you felt that warmth in your own heart. There's something magical about helping others, isn't there? It's a feeling that no amount of money can buy. And when Jake faced the ultimate temptation of immense wealth, we all held our breath. Would he choose riches or stay true to the values he'd learned? His decision reminds us that true happiness comes from living according to our principles, not from material possessions.

In the end, Jake's realisation about the note's true purpose mirrors our own journey through life. We're all given opportunities - some big, some small - to make a difference. The magic isn't in the opportunity itself, but in how we choose to use it. As you close this book, I hope you'll carry Jake's lessons with you, looking for those magical moments in your own life where you can make a positive impact.

So, what will you do with your own "magical money"? Whether it's your time, your talents, or your resources, you have the power to create magic in the world around you. Just like Jake, the choice is yours. And I can't wait to see what wonderful things you'll do with it.

www.ingramcontent.com/pod-product-compliance
Lightning Source LLC
Chambersburg PA
CBHW030429160726
47991CB00005B/1655